VietnamEazy

VietnamEazy

A Novel About Mothers, Daughters and Food

By Trami Nguyen Cron

Printed in the United States of America
FIRST EDITION ISBN 978-0986189890

WELLSTONE CENTER
in the Redwoods

Wellstone Books an imprint of the Wellstone Center in the Redwoods
858 Amigo Road Soquel, CA 95073
www.wellstoneredwoods.org
Distributed by Publishers Group West

This book is dedicated to my family.

Table of Contents

A Star

SAUTEED CRAB IN SECRET SAUCE
Cua Rang Sauce Cà Chua

4 Servings

INGREDIENTS:

Optional: A pot of oil for deep frying crab

2 tablespoons chili oil

1 teaspoon chopped garlic

9 ounces chicken broth

2 ounces ketchup

2 tablespoons chili sauce

1 teaspoon fish sauce

1/4 cup chopped lemongrass

1 Dungeness crab

1 1/2 tablespoons sugar

2 eggs

6 sliced red Fresno peppers

1 fried shallot

1 1/2 tablespoons green onions sliced into coins

4 sprigs cilantro

(Continued on next page)

Quarter the crab reserving the top shell. Optional step: Deep fry for four minutes.

Heat the chili oil in a wok, add garlic, and sauté until caramelized. Add chicken broth, ketchup, chili sauce, fish sauce and lemongrass and stir. Once the sauce comes to a boil, add the crab and toss in the sauce until the crab is hot and completely coated. Add sugar and bring to a boil, then add the egg and scramble. Garnish with the sliced peppers, fried shallots, green onion and cilantro.

Iknew I didn't belong. I glanced around the sprawling L.A. hotel ballroom, looking from face to face, and the same thought kept hitting me like a gong being pounded: "What am I even doing here?" I'd worked over the years to stamp out any hint of an accent. I could speak just fine, but I knew there was no way I had the look or the back story the producers of the reality show *Sliced and Diced* hoped to find. They had gathered their newest batch of two hundred wannabe star chefs, me among them, in the over-air-conditioned depths of the Los Angeles Hilton. No one could knock my wardrobe, it was true. I had wriggled into a black pencil skirt and black lace top revealing just enough cleavage. My long dark hair, almost black, was loosely curled to create those waterfall tiered waves. The camera would like me, but that didn't mean the producers would. I am a Vietnamese immigrant.

At barely five feet tall, I knew I was not tall enough for the *Sliced and Diced* producers. Given my lifelong love of food, I was not thin enough. My skin was not light enough. I was not dainty and pretty enough, at least not by Vietnamese standards. My saving grace was my large, double-creased, dark eyes. This Western feature is revered by most Asian women. Many opt for surgery to change their eyelids, creating a scar to mimic a crease on their upper lids. Some use Scotch tape at night to hold back their lids so that by morning they'll have the crease for at least a few hours. How they sleep with their eyelids taped back, I have no idea. Everyone in my family has the signature large eyes and double-creased lids. They say people who don't have the crease appear sly and untrustworthy.

Waiting in the cold hotel ballroom, my thoughts raced back to my conversation that morning with my mother, who was in fine form. She happily recounted what my stepfather had asked her when he found out I was trying out for the show: "Does she even know how to cook?" My mother then paused, as if delivering a punch line, and broke into cruel laughter.

"'You don't really need to know how to cook for those shows anyway,'" my mother continued happily, relaying what she claimed to have told my stepfather. "'Kieu knows enough. Besides, she will have me to help with her presentation.'"

My mother might as well have taken out a knife and plunged it into my back. That was her way. She could wield a knife on me, but she could never wield one on a show like *Sliced and Diced*. Nobody would understand a word she uttered. Back home in Vietnam, she was respected as an articulate woman who could write beautiful poems in the ancient Chinese style. Now in California she did not even have the ability to communicate with her youngest son about simple things like his college career plans. She spoke only a few words of English.

My mother's attacks always found their mark, but that morning for some reason I was able to ignore her. This was *my* day. I felt lucky. I muttered the appropriate half-hearted laugh in response, polite but dismissive, and moved on. Still, the story left me with misgivings that I filed away to be considered later. Could it possibly be true that even my stepfather didn't know I was a talented cook? How could that be? Growing up I would sometimes cook when Mom was not around. She ran a catering business out of our home and I was her only assistant. As an adult I created gourmet meals for the family when they came to California to visit. I had a momentary flash that maybe

Mom was so jealous, she made up the story to put me in my place and remind us both that she was the cook in the family. If anyone was going to be on TV, *she* should be the one, not me! I was shocked to find myself having such thoughts. It was the first time in my life I'd ever questioned my mother's motives. I was thirty-eight years old.

Was I seeing a rivalry play out that was another version, a kind of pale copy, of the tortured interplay between my mother and grandmother that ran through my childhood like the San Andreas Fault runs through California? When I was eight years old, living in Paris, Grandma took a bath and asked me to help scrub her back. She sat in the tub facing away from me and I slowly scrubbed the soft, white flesh on her back with a small washcloth while trying not to look at her other body parts. She noticed me trying not to look.

"Are your mother's breasts more saggy than mine?" she asked me suddenly.

I didn't know what to say. I had never seen my mother's breasts, but had seen my grandmother's many times. Grandma twisted around in the bathtub to meet my gaze and demand a reply. I was on the hot seat. Silence would have been disrespectful. If I told her I had never really thought about it, her pride would have been hurt to learn I had not studied her breasts in detail.

"Yes, Ngoại, Mom's breasts are more saggy," I said, scrubbing her back.

"I know," she agreed quickly, smiling triumphantly. "I've told your mother many times that she should take better care of them. After having only two children, her breasts are even saggier than old-lady Ngoại's breasts after five children."

I felt guilty about that conversation in the days that followed, and in fact feel guilty about it to this day. I did not protect my mom's breasts' honor. Where did my loyalties lie? With my mother, the mystery woman who gave birth to me, or to Ngoại, the woman who raised me? Or should I have simply told the truth, which was that as a kid such things were beyond me. I was far too young to have breasts of my own.

This was the kind of riddle from my past I'd have liked to sort through with my husband. For some couples a road trip is a chance to step back from the hectic daily grind and catch up on each other's lives. For me our six-hour drive down to L.A. for *Sliced and Diced* meant several hours of staring out the window as a deep male voice read from a book. My husband was not a man who had ever felt comfortable expressing his thoughts or feelings. He had a vast collection of audio books and listened to them all the time – on long trips, to and from work, even just popping out to the store. They were his means of escape. I'd often wondered what childhood calamity left him so withdrawn. I'd probed for answers, but to hear him tell it he had grown up in a home straight out of *Leave It to Beaver*. And the truth was, my in-laws had a lot in common with Ward and June Cleaver. Everything about their two-story home in upstate New York, where he grew up, seemed perfect. The only thing that left a mark in my memory was the basement. It was neat and equipped with a wide enough array of tools to build an entire house. I imagined John's father must have spent endless hours in that basement, tucked safely away from the family, removed from his wife, tinkering with his tools, the occasional whir of saws and drills only highlighting the absence of words and human connection.

I looked over at my computer-engineer husband and made my usual bid to prod him to open up to me. "Honey, if you could do anything and money was not an object, what would you do?" I asked him.

A flicker of annoyance passed over John's eyes. I had interrupted the calming monotone of the male narrator's voice. John reached for the pause button with what felt to me like exaggerated slowness. Even his movements struck me as tedious. I stared at his scabby, bloody fingertips, victims of his nail-biting habit, and waited for him to reply. I'd almost forgotten my question by the time he finally spoke up.

"I would be a counselor," he said, just so, and I was waiting to see where he might go with this promising beginning. But those five words represented his total outpouring.

I gestured with my right hand to encourage him to continue. He kept his eyes on the road, silent.

"Why?" I finally asked, trying not to show any annoyance.

"It would have been interesting," he said.

In the endless chess match that is marriage, he'd just check-mated me. I had only two options: continue pulling teeth without the proper dental equipment, or let him get back to his comfortable audio-book world. Fine. For him being stuck in the car together for six hours must have been torture enough without being forced to connect with his wife. Flashing the gracious smile of the defeated, I reached over and pressed the play button.

"Number thirty-nine, forty and forty-one!" came the announcement in the waiting room for *Sliced and Diced*. I felt steel bands of anxiety encircling me, knowing it was almost my turn to be called.

The woman who made the announcement was in her twenties, blonde and fit with that absent look of surfers and fashion models who don't really care but want you to think they might. She was probably some kind of intern the network hired for the cattle call. I could tell she took her job seriously as she glanced down to double-check her clipboard with a look of crisp efficiency. My pits felt suddenly sweaty and my stomach started to churn as if I had food poisoning. Mom and I both had this condition. Whenever we got too excited, we needed to run to the bathroom.

Hurrying off to find the ladies room, I spotted an African-American woman along the way who was still working on her five-page application right then and there. I couldn't believe it. I'd spent many long days laboring to make sure I had completed mine absolutely as well as I could. I couldn't take my eyes off this woman with her blonde hair, too-tight jeans, two-inch French manicured-tip fingernails and red pen squiggling away. I wondered what the theme of her show would be. I doubted it could be anywhere near as good as mine.

"Number fifty-seven, fifty-eight and fifty-nine!"

My turn! Before I could panic, I looked over at John for reassurance. He smiled and gave me a "You're OK" nod. Sometimes his calmness was just what I needed. My thoughts were veering wildly toward questions I should have settled well before that moment. Should I just be myself? Or should I create some flashy character who would grab the producers' attention? Someone impulsive and rude and charismatic? Someone who acted out and threw tantrums? No meek person was going to be selected for the show, that much was clear. Even contestants who didn't end up winning often landed their own shows if they were somehow big personalities or colorful or interesting. Why hadn't I thought all of this through beforehand?

I decided I'd have to come across as the Ruthless Asian Chick. The only memorable, successful Asian TV personality I could think of was Margaret Cho, who was crude and loud. She was never delicate. She was everything a Vietnamese woman should never be. I would work a Cho variation: I would be blunt, self-assured and bossy. In other words, I would be myself.

I walked into the small meeting room and there was the young woman I'd assumed was an intern, now sitting behind a table covered with a white table cloth. She motioned for me to sit down with a sweeping wave of her right hand, like a queen summoning the peasant to bow. I fought back a flinch and then eased into a smile. There was no way I was going to let this girl intimidate me. She glanced at my application, then looked up and fixed me with a stare that was both insolent and friendly.

"What is your show going to be?" she asked.

"*VietnamEazy*," I told her, a smile of pride breaking through. "Vietnamese food made easy with American ingredients."

I saw a quick twinkle pass her eyes. She motioned for me to stay in my chair while she grabbed her smartphone, stood up and left.

I was taken aback. I was not sure if she'd been daydreaming and wanted to send a quick text to her boyfriend suggesting a new move they should try in the bedroom as soon as possible or if I'd offended her so much that she couldn't stand to waste another second in my presence. Had she caught a whiff of my sweaty armpits? Oh no! My eyes danced around the small meeting space. I felt a fresh blast of machine-frozen air and wished I had a scarf. I love my scarves. If my neck is warm, I am warm. Ngoại always said to cover our necks in cold areas or we might get *courant d'air*, French for a draft of air. Every Vietnamese knew that this deadly wind attacks its victim, causing permanent or temporary paralysis or a crooked face.

I heard the door close quickly behind me and saw the girl coming back toward me in a hurry, trailed by an older man with thinning gray hair and a bland, distracted air. He grinned as he approached and stuck out his right hand.

"Tell me more about your show's concept," this producer said. "*VietnamEazy*, was it?"

I gave him a broad smile.

"Yes, exactly," I said. "The American audience is ready to learn to make Vietnamese food. I arrived in Kansas with my family when I was eleven. It was a challenge for my mom to find Vietnamese ingredients, so she developed a way to make authentic-tasting Vietnamese food with American ingredients that you can get in the supermarket. I've improved the recipes over the years and am really happy to be able to share them now."

He moved on to other questions about food and cooking. He asked what I did for a living and if I was able to leave my life for three months to tape the show, if I was fortunate enough to advance all the way through to the finals. I told him it was no problem at all, since I owned my own acupuncture clinic in Santa Cruz and could easily add another acupuncturist to see my clients while I lived out my dream.

"You will hear from us within twenty-four hours," he called back to me on his way out, leaving as quickly as he had arrived, still smiling with that amused look of discovery in his eyes. "Are you going to be around?"

Where else would I be?

"Yes!" I replied happily.

I thanked the blonde woman on my way out. She may be young, I thought to myself, smiling at her, but she was no dummy.

Our home in Saigon was the tallest and grandest on the street. Ngoại forbid us to go barefoot outside like all the other children. Sometimes Minh and I would wear our French-designed shoes just far enough down the street that Ngoại could no longer see us, and then pull them off. There was nothing like the freedom of bare feet. We didn't care about hurting ourselves. We didn't worry about catching deadly diseases. We just wanted to fit in with other kids and not get picked on because of our fancy clothes.

One day when we were playing, a neighbor girl slammed right into me by accident and sent me sprawling to the ground knee first. The jolt startled me. I sat down and realized that a brown piece of glass had pierced my left knee. Blood was everywhere. I looked up to find Minh standing over me, staring at the blood. I didn't feel any pain.

"Minh, get Ngoại," I told him.

He just stood there, unable to peel his eyes away from my knee.

"Get Ngoại!" I screamed.

He finally snapped out of his trance and ran as fast as he could to get Grandma. She came right away and kept repeating "*thôi chết rồi, thôi chết rồi* – this is death, this is death!" I felt cold rush over me and started to shake. Uncle Quốc, my mother's younger brother, held me in his arms and hopped on the back of his best friend Uncle Khôi's Honda motorcycle. They raced through the streets of Saigon to get me to a hospital. My next recollection was of being set on an operating table with bright lights over me as I stared up at Uncle Quốc's face. *Where is my mom? I want my mom. Why isn't she here?* Uncle Quốc held my hand as the doctor told him they had to sew my knee up. I spotted a long needle and had to look away. I kept my stare above me and felt nothing except the embrace of solitude even as I gripped my uncle's fingers in my left hand. After what seemed like a long time, it was over and the pain finally crept in. They moved me to a resting room where I waited for Mom to arrive. I fantasized about how she would run to me and hug and kiss me. She would tell me she felt so sorry for me. I would be in heaven with all the attention she would lavish on me.

I heard the quick clicking of platform heels and knew she had arrived. Mom came over to my bed with fear in her eyes. She wore a billowy yellow shirt, tight bell-bottom jeans, brown platform shoes and a big, brown hobo bag. Her hair was knotted back in a bun. She hovered over my bed and glanced at my knee. She did not hug me or kiss me. She did not touch me or even speak to me. I could only read her face, but was afraid to look into her eyes. Did I see love or disappointment? I couldn't tell. I was causing trouble for her and that thought hurt more than any pain I felt in my knee.

After a brief moment she motioned for Uncle Quốc, whose white-collared shirt was stained red with my blood, to leave the room with her. They stood in the hallway to discuss my case.

"They think she should be OK to walk again but they are not sure," I overheard him tell my mother. "Her nerves and tendons don't seem to be affected. You should have seen the white tendons!"

To this my mother had no reply.

"The hospital had no anesthesia, so they had to sew her up without any," Uncle continued, his voice rising for emphasis. "She is the strongest kid I know. She did not cry or shed a single tear."

Still nothing from my mother.

"I watched her face and lips turn from pink to purple to green," Uncle Quốc continued.

"They did a bad job sewing her up," I heard my mother say. "It's a mess. She will have a terrible scar forever. For a girl this is not good. If I had known sooner, I have a source who would have a supply of anesthesia. I could have gotten some for her."

"How could any of us have known sooner?" Uncle replied with obvious annoyance in his voice. "We tried to reach you as quickly as we could. You should have been around for your kids!"

"I was making a living at *Chợ Trời* (open air market)," Mom replied. "How can I do both?"

Everyone understood the situation was grave. After the fall of Saigon into Communist hands, the lack of medical supplies was dramatic. Women who had stayed home before the end of the war had to find ways to get out and make a living, trading personal possessions or working in the black market. Mom worked both the black market and the open-air market, selling French pharmaceuticals, electronics equipment and anything else she was able to purchase with the old Đồng currency before it became obsolete after September 22, 1975. Everything was changing, even how we talked to each other. In Vietnamese culture respecting family rank had always been extremely important. Growing up we were never allowed to point out the faults of our elders, not even our older brothers or sisters. That day marked the first time I ever heard Uncle Quốc speak to his older sister this way.

My proud half-smile as I walked back into the Los Angeles Hilton ballroom was all my husband needed to see to know it had gone well. He quickly broke into a wide smile, both relieved and thrilled, even if he did not begin to grasp how important this was for me, how much I loved *Sliced and Diced* and needed and wanted to be on the show, or how badly I wanted to share Vietnamese food with mainstream America and introduce our culture to a country that had been home to more than a million of us since 1975.

"They're going to call in the next twenty-four hours if they want me to come back," I told him.

He put his arm around my shoulder as we left the hotel lobby, his silence oddly fitting for a change. Three hours later came the call from the producer.

"We love the *VietnamEazy* idea!" he told me.

I understood that in the language of producers, they loved everything or they couldn't stand it. You were in or you were out. There was never any middle ground.

"See you at 9 a.m.," he said. "And come ready to cook."

My stomach went into freefall. No matter how excited I might have been, I was also terrified. The idea of an on-camera test made me feel like a nervous little girl, bound to disappoint. I could hear my mother's voice in my head telling me, "You're not so pretty that water will flow over walls for you! You will not marry a wealthy man, so make sure you get an education and can support yourself."

Or the time when I came home excited to show her my brilliant report card – all A's with just one A-minus. "What happened with the A-minus?" she asked, staring at me with her usual irritation and blanket disapproval. The giddy feeling of excitement and pride that had been coursing through me instantly vanished.

I often wonder how different a life I might have led if not for all the small rips and tears woven into the cloth of my psyche, created by my own mother with each cutting comment or hard, disapproving look. Is it possible to sew a beautiful Vietnamese *áo dài* (traditional skintight two-panel dress) with so many holes in the fabric? I gave up on ever becoming that perfect Vietnamese woman my mother apparently wished I would be. Perhaps this was why so many of us in-betweeners, born in Vietnam and raised in America, embraced American fashion, where baggy clothes and jeans with large holes were not only acceptable, but coveted.

Ideas buzzed through my head to prepare myself for my *Sliced and Diced* tryout. Which simple yet amazingly delicious dish should I make? This choice could shape my life forever. I summoned the look and taste of each dish as I flipped through the catalogue of recipes in my mind. I could smell my favorite one from childhood, a simple recipe Ngoại made for us as kids called *Mắm kho quẹt*. She would add about half a cup of pure fish sauce into a pan and reduce it until it was nothing but a fishy, crystallized salt mixed with black pepper and a little sugar. There was nothing like the smell of fish sauce cooking, pungent, fishy and wonderfully pleasing all at the same time. We would eat this unbelievable salty, sweet and savory paste with a bowl of hot steamed jasmine rice. Because of all the salt I had to drink glass after glass of water along with the dish. I remember asking for seconds and thirds until the rice swelled and my belly was so big I couldn't eat another bite.

It was a dish that from time to time I still craved, but it never tasted quite as good as it used to because now I ate it alone. I only whipped this dish out when my husband was away on a business trip and I found myself missing my family. John would have sent me packing from the smell of the dish alone. He could not stand the smell of fish sauce, so I only used it in tiny quantities when I cooked for him. When he was gone and I indulged my *Mắm kho quẹt* need, I took precautions. Often I aired out the house for three days afterward so that when John returned from his trip he would pick up no trace of my secret dish. That sounds funny: my secret dish. But that's what it was, at least a secret from my husband. Wait, that was an interesting idea: a *secret dish*. That would make a splash if I could announce my "secret dish" for the competition. But what could I cook that would live up to such a tantalizing description? I would have to think long and hard to find – no, I wouldn't. I had it: In my family we have our own recipe for crab, a simple yet unbelievably delicious crab dish served with fresh sliced French bread or steamed rice. I couldn't think of a more fitting choice for my first shot at making an impression on *Sliced and Diced*, a dish that would entice the judges and one that would tap into the fraught world of my family history, a dangerous decision, I was all too aware, but one well worth the risk if I was going to have a shot at winning this competition.

I was three years old when I first came to understand chaos. That was spring 1976 in Saigon. Mom took me by the hand, her arms so full of clothes she could hardly reach out to grab me, and shoved me into the back of a taxi. I was wearing the same light blue hand-knit sweater that I still recognize today in my baby pictures. I hated cars. My tiny body would stiffen up from the beginning of the ride all the way until the engine stopped. Mom took great delight in recounting tales of my childhood fear of car rides. She told people it was the grinding sounds of the motor that made me nervous, but she was wrong. It was the motion I didn't like. My mother never bothered to consider that possibility. She herself had never suffered from motion sickness, so why should I? For her the only logical explanation was the sound. I never received any sympathy for getting carsick. We didn't offer sympathy to family members. That would only encourage weakness. Denial and poking fun were the preferred ways of handling unpleasant things. My mother tried to cover up her embarrassment at my vulgar reaction to car rides by blaming my father's side, the dark-skinned "country" side.

"My little wine daughter, she's just a country girl who doesn't understand luxurious things like cars," she would say with a pompous laugh. "What a shame she will probably never be rich enough to own one if she doesn't learn to like them."

In Vietnam a pet name for a precious daughter is *con gái rượu*, or "wine daughter." Typically, fathers love drinking wine and prefer to be served by their daughters – boys are considered lazy and are not expected to serve. I didn't have a father to call me his wine daughter, but Mom used the expression in bitter mockery of him, as I understood all too well. Every time she called me wine daughter I knew she was cursing him and passing on to me, whether I wanted it or not, the angry, painful residue of their marriage.

My father was never a rich man. He was a teacher whose assets were a skillful tongue, a handsome face and artistic manners. That was more than enough to woo an innocent girl of nineteen like my mother. Grandma disapproved of their marriage, but Mom insisted, because she was in love. Ngoại never warmed to my father, never softened her harsh opinion of him, and his every misdeed pleased her, offering further proof that she had been correct in her assessment. On the day Saigon fell into Communist hands, April 30, 1975, my father deserted us. A lover of his had somehow found a way to have him added to her family list and so there he was on one of the helicopters lifting off from the American Embassy that chaotic, surreal, smoke-shrouded day. After his departure, Mom reluctantly moved back in with Ngoại. Instead of expressing sympathy for Mom's plight, Ngoại reminded her daily of her failure in her choice of a husband.

That day I put on a cloak of worry that I would never take off. I didn't know if I would see my brother Minh ever again. Whenever Mom and Ngoại disagreed, the topic of who got to keep my brother always came up. He was the first grandchild. He was a bright boy with big brown eyes. He was fiercely loyal to Ngoại and was clearly her favorite. I always knew this, but don't remember ever resenting him. I adored Minh. He was the only constant presence in the first three years of my life. No matter where we lived, he was always there. This time Ngoại won and I was alone with Mom in the taxi under all these clothes.

That particular car ride with my mother in spring 1976 will always stand out clearly in my memory. Mom, uncharacteristically, didn't make a single sound. As I replay the memories of that car ride now, I can see Mom's tears waiting for permission in the corners of her eyes. I feel a compassion for her in retrospect that at the time was beyond me, scared and bewildered as I was. I would never have thought of infuriating her by asking any questions – we were forbidden to ask questions – but I knew Mom had argued with her mother, Ngoại.

The direct translation of "Ngoại," the mother's mother, is "outside" grandmother. (A paternal grandmother is the "inside" grandmother.) In many ways Mom and Ngoại had always been on the outside – outside of their own families, outside of their fathers' affection and outside of each other's love. Now they were handing that legacy down to me.

I could barely see out the car window, so all I glimpsed were bellies and backs of people on bikes and three-wheeled rickshaws called *Xích Lô* zooming by. Thank God the window was rolled down on my side. It was hot and steamy in Saigon. The kisses of warm wind helped suppress the nausea welling up in my throat. A vendor on the street was yelling out with his Chinese accent "*Bánh Bao nóng ăn liền, ăn liền* – Hot buns eat now, eat now!" The smell of these hot minced pork, sausage and egg-filled steamed buns was my favorite. I loved peeling off the thin, sweet, outside layer of the large, doughy, milk-white bun and eating it first, then breaking it in half. With each bite I made sure I had enough salty meat and sweet dough to balance the flavors and texture. I always saved the egg for last. The chalky cooked yolk was like eating thick, creamy clouds.

I looked over at Mom to see if she had given the tears permission to flow, but she had not. There they remained, waiting. She now had a "planning" look on her face. Mom always knew what to do next. She gave directions to the driver, leaned back and finally looked over at me, her youngest child, the unplanned child. Mom had jet black hair, long and slightly wavy, that fell down onto her waist like beautiful, thick, black silk. Her face was marked by a high-bridge nose, a preferred European feature in Vietnamese women. She had large brown, sparkling eyes, light skin and plump lips. She had a thin, long waist, large breasts and a perfect European profile. She was the most beautiful woman I knew.

I sat as still as I could, trying not to provoke her while trying to control my stomach and throat. The cloying smell of ripe car leather did not help. I swallowed the hot, wet air to control the nausea that came and went of its own will. I tried to stick my face and nose out the window to get some air. Oh God, would we ever get there? Wherever there was? My breathing grew faster and shallower. I lifted my nose, trying to get more fresh air. I prayed I would not throw up. This would only provoke her more. I could not cause trouble for her, not then, not ever.

Then suddenly the car stopped. All I could think was "Get out, get out" but I didn't know how to open the car door. I had to wait, wait for Mom to pay the driver, wait for her to gather all the clothes, wait for her to release me. At last I was out of the car. I felt the sun on my face and the solid ground under my feet again. I gave one last shudder as my stomach slowly stopped churning. A sense of great relief washed over me, although in some ways I would never move beyond that suffocating experience. All it takes is a whiff of diesel fumes or car leather to return me to that day. When I bought a new car a few years ago, I had to air it out for days to exorcise the stench before I could drive it.

Whenever I made my favorite crab dish for my Vietnamese friends, they would ooh and aah and beg me for the recipe. It was literally finger-lickin' good. I told them it was my mom's secret recipe and I could never reveal it or she would disown me. They readily accepted this explanation. For us, any threat to one's family honor was always an acceptable excuse whenever one wanted to gracefully decline an offer. The truth was I didn't want to reveal the recipe because I wanted it to be special. My Vietnamese friends could only eat that dish when they invited me to make it for them.

Without a real name for the dish, my friends called it *Cua Rang Me* (Sauteed Crab in Tamarind Sauce). I never corrected them, but actually the dish didn't even contain any tamarind. I chuckled to myself each time they said *Cua Rang Me*. A few attempts were made to duplicate my recipe. They failed. They would always fail. I was well trained to keep bigger secrets, so keeping a recipe under wraps was second nature.

Ngoại always loved to be the center of attention. She was pretty, alluring, seductive. Our family said she was the Liz Taylor of Vietnam. Her voice was decent enough that she would get paid to work as a lounge singer in a small club in Saigon a few nights a week. She purposely never took on the official title of Professional Singer, preferring to be seen only as an invited special guest of the lounge. A professional singer title, *Con Ca Sĩ*, carried with it connotations of classlessness and promiscuity, almost verging on prostitution. *Con* used in this context was considered disrespectful. This was where the conflicting Vietnamese culture confused me. I could only compare it to the geisha of Japan. Professional singers were envied and loved, yet at the same time they were not held in high regard. Children were never encouraged to be singers. Having a college education was considered the key to gaining respect. Pursuits like art or music were never fully acceptable. Yet most of my Vietnamese friends loved karaoke, secretly longing to be on stage singing instead of hiding behind their computer desks at Cisco.

Ngoại was a single mother raising Mom on her own while working as a secretary at a local factory during the day. She easily secured this position with her sixth-grade education, a rarity for women of her generation, as well as her typing skills, gentle manner and good looks. She made enough money to live on her own and have a maid to help take care of Mom.

She met her second husband one night after she had performed her favorite song. He was the mayor of a small village near Hanoi, and he gave her a huge bouquet of flowers as she stepped off the stage. He was wealthy enough, handsome, charming and tall. For Vietnamese men, being tall was the most important physical trait. A short man, no matter how successful, would always be mocked behind his back. The mayor came to the club every night she sang. She quickly fell into his arms and he married her a few months later. Their courtship was quick as he was quite the catch and she was afraid he might get snatched up by someone else. But all she knew of him was whatever he told her. He was significantly older than she was, but it was not unusual then for men to take very young brides. She never questioned why she didn't get to meet his family or have a formal wedding ceremony. Society already considered her damaged goods after a divorce and a child. She was glad that she now had a man who could take care of her. She remained in her town while he traveled back and forth. She had a few secrets, too, conveniently forgetting to tell him about her son, Mom's younger brother, for one.

Mom told me stories about Ngoại and how she loved being married to her new husband. For her he was the epitome of a man. He was good looking, articulate, educated in French schools and seemingly powerful. He and his friends would refer to each other as *moi* and *toi*, the French pronouns of me and you, which was typical of the educated class. He had nightly political meetings away from the house.

Mom respected him because whenever Ngoại would get out of line with her demands he would "give her a smack." That's what they called it. In Vietnamese families it was not unusual for men to beat their wives. I remember as a kid hearing our neighbors get into physical brawls all the time. No one was too alarmed by this. They might pause to listen, just to make sure it was not some real emergency. If it sounded like the usual arguments, throwing of things and beatings, everyone went on with their lives. If the woman was well liked, they would feel sorry for her and would check in on her the next morning and give her iodine and eucalyptus oil to salve her wounds. They would criticize the husband for being so unnecessarily mean. If she was not well liked, then they would say "*Đáng đời lắm.*

Cho ông dạy nó − She deserved it. Let her husband teach her."

Ngoại and her husband would have these arguments at the end of every month. That was when they would run out of money. She didn't have the best money management skills. She would spend all the money he had given her for the month on clothes, jewelry, gifts and other fineries to impress her friends. She rationalized this by telling herself that he spent his money on drinking and other women. To her thinking, his money rightfully belonged to her. So besides being upset about not having enough money to pay her creditors, she sometimes added bouts of jealousy. She'd cry and beat her chest while reminding him how much she loved him and sacrificed herself to allow him to run around with other women. She had a gift for the dramatic. She was able to cry and make hacking and vomiting sounds on command. He usually yielded to her theatrics. He might not have been convinced, but who would want to witness the same awful scene unfold on a monthly basis?

As for his behavior, it was accepted for men to be philanderers. That was considered part of their male nature, *phóng khoáng*, or free-spirited. It was a quality to be admired in a man so long as he still took care of his wife and children at home. When Ngoại's demands were not met, she'd take her disappointment out on her first child, whose mere sight fueled her fire. She used to make Mom recite her poetry homework every night. If Mom failed to have it memorized, she was banished to the kitchen until she got it. Kitchens were usually built separately from the main house, out in the courtyard, to prevent the smoke from infiltrating the house.

Sitting in the dark on the cement floor with just a kerosene lamp to keep her company terrified Mom. So instead of concentrating on her homework, in the flickering light she would imagine ghosts and spirits lurking behind every pot and pan. This fertile imagination distracted her from the words on the page. After a few hours Ngoại would check in on her and if she had failed to memorize the required poems, she found herself sleeping on the cement floor.

Those were the good nights. The bad ones involved spankings with a feather duster made from a long woven rattan stick with layers of brown chicken feathers glued to one end. Ngoại would hit Mom from her legs to her buttocks to her arms. The face was always avoided. That would have been crossing a line: To hit a person in the face was considered abuse. The spanking was usually accompanied by name-calling and insults, all of it heard by the neighbors. On these nights it was as if Grandma was possessed by demons while anger spewed out of her. These ghosts were all too real for Mom.

"You are stupid!"

"You are a whore!"

"You are worthless!"

"I should have never given birth to you!"

The next morning, the old lady next door would catch Mom on her way to school to check her wounds, put iodine on them and softly shake her head back and forth. "You didn't deserve it, child," she would assure her. "Misses got so angry. You didn't deserve it."

Mom appreciated the old woman's soothing words. She recounted these stories to me over and over, giving them the passion and tone required to help a listener feel you were there. I focused on her words until I had every scene memorized, including the one where she was beaten for a record-breaking time from sundown to sunup, until the bamboo stick splintered into skinny pieces and Ngoại had to grab whatever else she could find to continue the spankings. No adult ever intervened. No one ever called authorities.

Ngoại's husband was never home when these beatings occurred. Her anger usually boiled over when he went away on business trips. One day, when there was a knock on the door, Ngoại thought her husband had forgotten his keys. Although irritated, she managed to pull herself together to greet him with her charming smile. But to her surprise, it wasn't him. It was an older woman dressed in country garb with six children behind her. She was his first wife from the countryside.

They used to call Hollywood a dream factory, and that was just what came to mind when I was dropped off outside one of the former big studios and walked in through the gate, past cavernous structures in which a set could have been created to evoke almost any reality. Finally I was inside the right large warehouse, staring at an expanse of mini-kitchens, row after row of sinks and counters and stoves. Kitchen utensils, knives, cutting boards, pots and pans – they were all off to the side, patiently waiting to see some action. I was greeted by a young man with blond hair and kind eyes who asked me to turn in my twenty-page signed contract of do's and don'ts and directed me toward the back. It was then that I got a look at my competition. There were thirty of us waiting to snatch up the opportunity of a lifetime to become the new star on *Sliced and Diced.*

I kept my gaze straight ahead, seemingly nonchalant, as I relied on my peripheral vision to check everyone out. It was critical to come across as if I couldn't have cared less about any of them. I wanted them to know it didn't matter what any of them were doing because the star had arrived. I wore a fitted, orange sleeveless dress with pockets that flared slightly from the waist. I had my signature thirty-two-inch Mikimoto pearls around my neck like religious Buddhist beads. I had on comfortable black pumps this time. I carried a large Gucci tote bag with all my cooking knives and other necessities, including an extra pair of black, flat ballet-inspired shoes, just in case.

I was thrilled to see only one other Asian girl. She looked about thirty and was heavier set, a sign of a real food lover, and definitely not Vietnamese. My guess was she was Chinese. I was not concerned about her.

I saw a really young guy, about twenty-five with Elvis hair. This was his way of being unique. Fine, I'd fall for that. But could he cook and speak on camera at the same time? And what was his special point of view? Let me guess, he could make a banana PB&J sandwich?

I tried to remind myself never to underestimate the young. They have energy and life in them that can inspire an audience. I have been inspired by TV chefs like Bobby Flay and Rachel Ray, who were quite young when they began to build their audiences. Look at them now. They practically own their own TV networks.

Someone came around and gave me my number. Number eight. My lucky number. I was still staring at that lucky "8" in my hand when the loudspeakers crackled with an announcement from the director.

"You know the drill," he said. "This is your moment. There are thirty of you now. Only twelve will make it to the show. Keep your blades sharp."

I avoided eye contact. I didn't need to make friends with Elvis or the Chinese girl. I didn't need to make friends with anyone. Like all the contestants, I had a cardboard box full of ingredients awaiting me. This contest was a sprint. We had twenty-five minutes to prep, twenty-five minutes to cook and three minutes to present our dishes on camera. I picked up my cardboard box and walked toward one of the counters.

Garlic. Check.

Onions. Check.

Lettuce. Check

Cracked and cleaned cooked crab. No! There was crab, but it hadn't been prepared as I'd asked. Cracking and cleaning the crab would add about five minutes to my prep time. I was annoyed, but quickly regained my calm. Just a little extra hurdle. I knew I could still make this work.

French bread. Check.

Vegetable oil. Check.

Sugar, ketchup, tomato paste, red pepper flakes, salt and pepper. Check.

Where was my lemongrass? There was no chopped lemongrass? It was the key ingredient to the dish. Otherwise it might as well be called Chef Boyardee Crab.

I debated my options. I didn't want to be labeled as difficult right at the outset, so I decided not to make an issue of the oversight. I became more and more nervous and my armpits started to feel a little warm. I needed to shift my focus away from this mishap and concentrate on my three-minute presentation.

The first round of contestants completed their prep time and moved on to their cooking segment. That meant it was my turn as part of the second group of contestants. I chopped my onions into little cubes with ease. Mom taught me how to chop onions like a pro, without ever cutting my finger. The trick was using the knuckle from my left middle finger as a guide for the knife with each chop. I ran my knife under tap water every so often to wash the onion juice from the blade so my eyes would not tear up and make my mascara run. I chopped the garlic, washed the lettuce and opened the canned chicken broth. I cut, cracked and cleaned that cooked crab in four minutes flat. I'd made this dish many times, so it came easily to me. My twenty-five minutes were up!

I waited off to the side while they cleaned the kitchen from the previous five contestants. I could smell the aroma of curry in the air. There was my competition. I homed in on a nice-looking, older Indian woman dressed in a silk sari of beautiful bright pink woven with gold threads to make a sharp pattern trimming the edges of the fabric.

We sure needed an Indian chef on TV. That was a cuisine that was still a mystery to me. I had never explored how to make Indian dishes from scratch, thinking it was too difficult. Sure, we had our versions of curries in Vietnamese food, but they were nothing like the Chicken Tikka Masala or Saag Paneer we usually ordered from restaurants. Sometimes I bought prepared Indian sauces in jars at the grocery store, but they always tasted off, so I would add fish sauce to make them a little *VietnamEazy*.

Cooking Shift No. 2 was now up! Our every move would be scrutinized by judges as if we were on camera. I ended up with Stan, a stocky man with stubby fingers. He watched me closely and kept asking me questions to gauge my cooking knowledge and also my ability to think on my feet. It was like being on *Iron Chef* with constant jarring interruptions.

I started by sweating my onions and garlic in a large pan until they were translucent. I explained that all these ingredients could be purchased in any American grocery store. Then I added all the remaining ingredients except for the crab. At that moment I decided to reach into my dress pocket to pull out a little plastic bag of chopped lemongrass. Stan-the-judge's eyes lit up. I flashed a confident smile

"One is always prepared to bring a little *VietnamEazy* to every dish," I told him.

I opened the bag and delicately used the tips of my fingers to sprinkle the lemongrass into the pan as though I were concocting a potion that needed a pinch of magic dust. I stirred it in and added the crab. There were only three minutes left to plate and present the dish. I quickly cut up a few slices of French bread and placed individual lettuce leaves on a large platter, spread out like a big fan. With my perfectly manicured natural nails front and center, I carefully arranged each crab piece on top of the lettuce. I placed three slices of lightly toasted bread to the left side like lotus petals to finish each plate.

I took a risk with the lemongrass. Thank God it paid off. It was an element that Stan did not expect, but I did not get disqualified because that ingredient was in my recipe. The judge motioned for me to bring my plate toward the camera section. He nodded to me with a smile of approval and admiration that hit me like a burst of sunshine on a cloudy day. I was going to need all the confidence I could get for my three-minute on-camera test.

Those three minutes could change everything for me. Often while working at my acupuncture clinic, I'd let myself dream about a scenario just like this. A reality show was just the excitement I needed. In my late twenties I received a diagnosis of mild attention deficit disorder of the inattentive type. My symptoms were completely manageable without any medication. But I did have a bottle of Ritalin in the back of my makeup drawer just in case. Those pills helped me get through my fifteen-hour flights from San Francisco to Paris once a year to visit Ngoại. I inherited this condition from Mom. I loved our active conversations as we hopped from topic to topic, leaving our families still contemplating an earlier point we'd raised. It bothered them to no end, but to us it felt perfectly natural. We communicated on a level of organized chaos. There was no one else I knew who could do this with me. When speaking with friends, colleagues and patients, I had to refrain from letting myself go and instead maintained an exterior calm to hide the mania that was roiling inside. I chose to pursue a career as an acupuncturist to force myself to remain quiet for eight hours a day, four days a week. It was therapeutic to listen to yoga music under dim lights while inserting little needles into my patients.

Now I was facing bright lights, three camera operators, one director and a bunch of miscellaneous people doing I did not know what. I should have taken my pill today. Why didn't I think of that? Then again, I avoided taking those calming pills most of the time because they muted my personality. I was going to need that today!

"Now Kieu, we would like for you to say a little about what you've prepared," the director coached me. "Don't forget to tell us stories about how you came up with the dish."

I was still debating if I should tell a wonderful childhood story about cooking with Ngoại. I never cooked with my grandma because the maids did all the cooking. In Vietnam, I barely entered the kitchen. Or should I tell them I learned how to cook because I worked in my family's restaurant beside my mom since I was twelve? I was there every day after school until closing. Sometimes when things were slow, I walked next door to the public library to read comic books. That was how I learned English. The pictures and word bubbles helped me understand this new language faster than I realized: After six months of reading comic books about fighting the evils of the world, I casually picked up a book about Ramona Quimby by Beverly Cleary that had been left behind on the little table by a blonde girl with her mom. And that was that. I abandoned comic books forever. I loved reading stories about this spunky six-year-old American girl whose mind ran as free as the Huggins' family dog, Ribsy. Although I was older than the Ramona character, it was nice to live out a little bit of a childhood that had passed me by.

"Miss Kieu, are you ready?"

"Yes, I am," I said.

I held my plate of sautéed crab, smiled and looked straight at the camera.

"Action!" said the director.

"Hi, my name is Kieu. I'm going to show you how to make an amazing Vietnamese crab dish that will leave your friends and family wondering what's your secret!" I said, smiling and holding the plate a little higher toward the cameraman to my right, inviting him to zoom in on the plate.

"If Vietnamese food sounds intimidating to you, don't worry," I said brightly. "We are going to make it *VietnamEazy* for you!"

I made sure to emphasize and stretch out the final syllables – eee-zee.

"You can get all the ingredients we are going to use right at your local supermarket," I added.

I dumped all the prep ingredients except the crab into a large pan with the hot oil.

"My family migrated to Kansas in the early 1980s," I said. "Needless to say, there were no Asian supermarkets around for my Mom to buy her ingredients. So she had to get creative and made us amazing, authentic dishes with ingredients we could find at any grocery store."

Looking straight at the camera I gave it my best Midwestern twang.

"Yes, believe it or not, I used to speak English with a Kansas accent, y'all."

OK, maybe people in Kansas don't say "y'all." But they don't know that in L.A.! I paused for comic effect then continued, holding up the bowl of chopped lemongrass.

"The most important ingredient in this dish is lemongrass," I said. "If you cannot find fresh ones, you can get them already chopped up in a jar in the foreign food section."

I turned to the deep pan and threw in the crab.

"Once the sauce is ready, we toss in the cooked crab that your butcher has nicely cleaned and cracked for you, then stir."

The time tracker was holding out the "30 seconds" sign to me. I held up the completed plate to the camera once more and smiled for my big finish.

"And here it is all done, a delicious plate of Crab Sautéed in a *VietnamEazy* Secret Sauce. The next time you think Vietnamese food is hard? Think easy. I'm Kieu and I look forward to making your next culinary adventure *VietnamEazy*."

2

Virtues

FEMININE SALAD
Gỏi Phụ Nữ

This salad is composed of many ingredients, requiring four different preparations to achieve visual appeal and the perfect balance of texture and taste. But it is easy and fast to prepare and is a great salad to make for neighbors or friends on a warm summer day. Your guests will love the fresh, crispy taste of this salad before a barbecue or nighttime get-together.

For this recipe you will need carrot, garlic, bean sprouts (washed and crispy), crispy shallots (store bought or freshly fried), roasted peanuts, chicken breast, herbs (mint, fresh basil and perilla leaves), chili paste (Sambal Oelek brand) and fish sauce.

3-5 Servings

Dressing ingredients:

6 tablespoons fish sauce
6 garlic cloves
6 limes, juiced
1 cup water
4 tablespoons sugar
1/2 to 1 tablespoon chili paste
(Continued on next page)

Combine fish sauce, five cloves of minced garlic, most of the lime juice (reserve a small amount and set aside) and the water and sugar in a saucepan and place over medium heat. Stir well and cook until just before boiling point is reached. Allow the dressing to cool, then pour it into a small serving bowl. Add one finely chopped clove of garlic and stir in the leftover lime juice and ½ tablespoon of the chili paste. Taste and add more chili paste if desired.

SALAD INGREDIENTS:

1 tablespoon olive oil
1/2 cup carrot
1 pound bean sprouts
1 pound cooked and shredded chicken
1/4 cup fresh basil
6 perilla leaves
1/4 cup mint leaves
2 teaspoons roasted peanuts
Optional: crispy fried shallots

Boil chicken breast until firmly cooked and then allow to cool before shredding into thin noodle-like pieces. Add salt and pepper to taste.

Chiffonade basil, mint and perilla leaves and combine with carrots and bean sprouts in a large salad bowl.

Add most of the dressing and toss thoroughly. Add more dressing if required. Sprinkle the salad with roasted peanuts and crispy shallots for added flavor.

My husband saw the incoming call flashing on my iPhone and hollered for me to come in from the balcony where I was watering plants. We stood there staring at the phone as if it might explode if we breathed too loudly. Finally I overcame my nerves and took the call.

"Congratulations!" a jolly producer called out, sounding as if he'd just sucked down some helium. "You are one of our twelve finalists to get on *Sliced and Diced*! Well, actually, you were thirteenth, but one of the other contestants had a –"

I was too stunned to listen. The only way I had kept my composure through the interviews and screen tests and awkward waiting-room encounters with other contestants was to cling to my certainty that they would never, ever choose me. Now they had. My world flipped upside down. My fate was to be a good wife to my husband and to take pride in his accomplishments, not my own. That was the way I was raised. That was the way generations of Vietnamese women had been raised. Who was I to buck that system? Who was I to hope to change my fate?

"Thirteenth?" I stammered weakly, realizing I'd better say something to the producer on the phone.

He laughed.

"No, no – you're twelfth. You made it!"

Why is it that when you try your hardest to stop the tears from flowing, they only gush more?

"Thank you," I said faintly, wanting to kick myself for sounding like a little girl.

The producer prattled on, relaying the logistics of what would happen next. He mentioned that he would be sending the details along in an email, so I knew I didn't have to try too hard to make sense of what he was saying. How could I make sense of anything?

There are four feminine virtues a Vietnamese woman must possess: *Công, Dung, Ngôn* and *Hạnh*. Be skillful, be beautiful, be eloquent, be virtuous. A Vietnamese woman has no choice but to accept the fate she is given by God. She can complain about that fate and get sympathy for it, but nothing more. She definitely cannot change it.

Fate was biased. A man could attempt to change the winds. He could do his utmost to shift the direction of his life if he wished. If he succeeded, he would be congratulated. "Truthfully, fate is only about 80 percent of life!" would come the pronouncement. "You can change the other 20 percent if you really want." If he fell short of his goal, well that was fate, wasn't it?

If a woman successfully changed the outcome of her ill-fated life, then it was just meant to be. Fate intended that for her all along. It wasn't because of something she did to escape its grips. And upon observing her physical traits, ah ha! It was ordained in her features to succeed.

My ex-mother-in-law never really cared for me. She thought I was too fat for her son, the doctor. Since he insisted on marrying me, she made sure to have my star charts read by a Vietnamese astrologer who deemed that our signs were compatible. She reluctantly accepted me as her future daughter-in-law only because I have a nose that was rather round at the tip. This was a sign that I would be rich.

Thank goodness I didn't opt for a nose job to slim out the tip of my nose and raise its bridge as so many Asian women do. The desire for this perfect feature has sent many girls to the operating table. Before the surgery the others would criticize the woman for having an unattractive flat or big nose. After the surgery they would talk behind her back, whispering and giving knowing looks that she had undergone surgery, clucking that her new attractiveness was bought and unnatural. You could never win.

For us, learning to love yourself didn't exist as a concept. Loving yourself meant you were selfish and self-centered. You would be violating the fourth admirable attribute, *Hạnh*.

To live for others and to please them was your duty, a duty drilled into us from an early age. As a teenager I was not allowed to go out often with my friends. If I planned to go to the movies on a Saturday, I would have to do extra chores, being extra cheerful and helpful with Mom to justify asking permission to go out with my friends. I'd wait until Saturday morning, when Mom seemed to be in a good mood, to plead my case.

"Mom, may I go to the movies with my friends tonight?" I asked sheepishly.

"What?" she barked. "*Đi đâu* – Go where?"

From her tone I knew I was in deep trouble. I wished I could take the question back. If I could, maybe that vicious look she was giving me would vanish from her face. I lowered my voice to answer her while avoiding looking into her big, dark eyes.

"To the movies," I stated as evenly as I could.

"Again?" she fired right back at me.

Her face was hard as stone as she put me in my place.

"You always want to go play around," she carried on. "You don't care about this family. Do you think this is a hotel? You should spend your time studying and tidying up the house!"

I bowed my head and bravely defended myself.

"I've only been out once with my friends! That was five months ago!" I protested.

OK, not really. I was such a coward, I could only voice such a brave response to her in the peace and quiet of my own thoughts. I never dared speak aloud such words to my mother. Instead, I clenched my jaw to hold back the tears of indignation. If she saw me cry, things would only get worse. I stood there until she dismissed me by turning her body away from me and returning her attention to watching Hong Kong kung fu movies, dubbed in Vietnamese. That was the end of the conversation. I went from being the model daughter all week to being an ungrateful, uncaring and shameful human being. I was fourteen.

Was she aware of the impact such a simple conversation would have on my life? Did she ever replay her memories of her own childhood, back to that time when she swore on the mountaintop of Shaolin Temple that she would never treat her children the way Ngoại treated her?

Mom had an active imagination as a child. To escape her daily life, she became a huge fan of martial arts books. Her favorites were written by a former Chinese newspaperman named Louis Cha, who wrote under the pen name Jin Young, or Kim Dung as he was commonly known. His books were packed with action and adventure and sold more than one hundred million copies worldwide. They explored human failings and constructed the moral foundations of many young people from her generation to mine. Within the pages of these books Mom found love and developed her sense of heroism.

In fact, these books were the best friends my mother had as a girl. Whenever she fell into a mood of thinking life was unfair, she would dream of climbing up to the top of Mount Song to live with Buddhist monks at the Shaolin Monastery, founded in the fifth century, and learn the ways of kung fu. After she had learned all the secrets of the masters, she would come down from the mountain and save the world from all that was unjust. She used to act out the action scenes in her sleep. She jumped around, kicking and fighting so much the mosquito nets on her four-poster bed fell over. Spanking and scolding soon followed those action-packed nights. That was when she swore never to hit her own children.

The philosophies from Dung's books shaped my mother's morals and world view throughout her life. This is probably true of many Chinese and Vietnamese youth of her time, and of my generation as well. We embraced Dung's philosophy of good vs. evil. Of how the truth will reveal itself one day. Of taking on suffering alone. Of protecting the weak. Of never explaining our actions. Of searching for our one true love. Of accepting that suffering is simply a part of life.

Mom never physically hurt us. She kept us in line by sending fear and disapproval surging out through her eyes. She had this way of widening her eyes so big you could see the white all around her dark irises. Her nose flared and we knew to stop whatever we were doing instantly. In place of whips to split our flesh apart, she used her big eyes and cutting words to tear through us.

Upon arriving at the television studio in New York City I was greeted by my new housemates, otherwise known as the competition. There were cameras everywhere capturing our every move. Thus it began. I put on my performance face and straightened my posture. I knew I looked good in my navy blue shift dress with capped sleeves, comfortable three-inch black pumps and 32D, back-fat suppressing bra. Everyone had drinks in their hands. To calm their nerves, I imagined. I was offered some Champagne but declined with a faint smile. I am allergic to alcohol. This is God's gift to many people of Asian descent.

I sized up my competition while smiling at them and shaking the men's hands and giving the women the appropriate three-second hugs. I could tell some were not huggers. I was not a hugger, either, but I wanted to throw them off. I knew from previous shows that it was best to play nice with everyone because you never knew who might become your teammate during one of the challenges, and there was always time later to turn people into enemies. I noticed Elvis sitting in the corner with his smartphone. So he made the show. Interesting. I slowly zigzagged over to him, acting as if I were headed somewhere else and had run into him by accident, then extended my hand.

"Hi, I'm Kieu," I said and waited for him to look up. Then I kept waiting. And kept waiting. I wondered if a camera in some corner was capturing my growing look of awkwardness. Elvis was thumbing his way through a text and clearly in no hurry to interrupt his progress.

"Hi, I'm Jay," he said, finally glancing up. "I saw you at the tryout."

So he *was* a straight shooter. I liked that.

"And I saw you," I said, a smile hovering at the corners of my lips.

Jay, it turned out, was a twenty-six-year-old working as an executive chef in a small restaurant in Dallas. His show was about giving a unique twist to traditional recipes. He was confident and articulate. I was impressed. I was also glad when our conversation was cut short by the host of the show.

"Welcome, everyone to *Sliced and Diced!*" the host called out.

He waited out a smattering of applause from the obvious butt-kissers among the contestants, and then flashed a wolfish smile.

"From now on you are no longer allowed to use your phones unless it is authorized by our producers," he announced, prompting a chorus of groans. "Those are the rules. Say bye-bye!"

Elvis' face crumpled into a look of extreme agony as his phone was wrenched from his hand. I did not have time to gloat. We all had to search our bags and pockets for our phones and hand them over as solemnly as possible, as if we were naughty children being punished. My iPhone is an extension of me. I was sure the separation anxiety and withdrawal pains from giving it up for the length of the competition – up to three months – would be a lot tougher than being away from my family.

"I am your host, Peter," he continued, pausing to see if he could milk a little more applause out of the moment. No luck on that front. The butt-kissers were chastened. Peter looked the part, that was for sure. He was a blonde man in his late thirties, handsome bordering on pretty, with a British accent and stylish spiky hair. He was the new host, just announced. His predecessor had been mysteriously dumped. Rumors circulated about a scandal involving fold-up lawn chairs, circus performers and Cheese Whiz, but the details shifted with each telling.

"Are you ready for your first challenge?" Peter intoned, hands clasped in front of his waist to highlight his perfect posture.

Every contestant but one – me! – gasped. They should have seen this coming. It was like a predictable plot twist in a scary movie: You had to know, if you watched enough reality TV, that they were going to try to catch you off-guard early with a shift in the routine. It was practically part of the routine. Silence settled over the room like a heavy sheet, but I was not fazed in the least. I had arrived the night before and got a good night's sleep before coming to the studio so I would be more than ready for whatever came. I'd heard talk of most of the others carousing until late.

"Today we would like you to cook a dish that represents you," Peter said, leaning on the last word like a life raft. "It can be anything you want it to be!"

Nervous buzzing filled the room again.

"You have one hour to prepare your dish and present it on camera to our panel of judges!"

Peter introduced the three judges and continued with the explanation on the rules of engagement. I listened attentively. Some of the contestants had clarification questions. Someone always had questions. This annoyed me. I wanted to get to my dish. Peter answered all the questions and then paused for emphasis before making one last statement for the cameras, smiling smugly and pausing for a long three-count.

"And two of you will be eliminated today!" he pronounced.

That was a new one for this show. They'd never axed *two* contestants right out of the gate like this before. Even I was shocked. Still, I did not put my hand to my chest or cover my mouth in astonishment, the way some of the women did. It was no surprise to have more drama thrown at us and no help to dwell on the latest twist. I was not worried about being eliminated this round. It was not going to happen. I had come prepared and knew exactly what to make. My mom's own creation, Vietnamese Feminine Salad. I picked this recipe because I was able to tell an interesting story about it. It entailed a lot of knife work but simple cooking techniques. I had practiced it for weeks before coming on the show and knew I could finish it in thirty minutes, no problem.

I put on the required white apron with the red *Sliced and Diced* lettering at the top and changed into the flats I always carried with me, dropping me from five-five to a mere five foot one. On almost any other occasion this sudden change in height would have left me feeling self-conscious and flustered, but not this time. Right then it did not matter to me how tall or short I was. Nothing mattered except that I was ready to go. I was ready to charm the hell out of them, a mantra I kept repeating to myself as we stepped over to the next stage, where twelve professional kitchen stations were set up.

"You have ten minutes to familiarize yourself with the pantry and collect all your ingredients," Peter told us.

Then he told us again – and again and again. As I was discovering, filming these shows required a lot of retakes. A one-hour show required dozens of hours of taping. I was anxious to get started.

"Get ready?" Long pause.

"Go!" exclaimed Peter.

The mad rush began. Almost everyone raced to the pantry, refrigerator and spice racks. Some ran to claim a cooking station, although there was one for everyone and they were all identical. It was hilarious, watching contestants dash madly, like cockroaches scurrying every which way when you turn on the lights. There were camera operators all over the place, capturing everything that happened, and I had to give one or two other contestants a gentle little forearm shiver to clear space as I moved around the kitchen like a ninja, quick as the wind but balanced and light on my feet.

I collected my fresh ingredients and herbs and spices and rushed to my cooking station. One of the first things I did was fire up a pan with deep-frying oil to fry my thin slices of sweet potato, and it was comforting to hear and smell the oil heating up. I pulled out my chef's knife to quickly julienne and chiffonade all my ingredients. Unlike professionally trained chefs with a full passel of knives, Vietnamese home cooks relied on cleavers. The rectangular-shaped blade is used for slicing, chopping, mincing and pounding. The handle is also used for pounding or for breaking hard shells like a hammer. We didn't need special tools for special tasks. One big, sharp cleaver and that was about it. Even professional chefs such as Martin Yan, my idol from the PBS show *Yan Can Cook*, used a single cleaver to do everything from thinly slicing a cucumber to deboning a whole chicken.

Personally I never liked using a cleaver. They looked clunky to me and, frankly, scary. I did not even own one. When Mom came to visit, she kept telling me that without a cleaver I did not have a real kitchen. I did not get offended by her attitude. I enjoyed the reminder to us both that I am not my mother. She loved her cleaver. I loved my knives. That's why I didn't much like cooking in other people's kitchens. I hated to do without my own knives. I could judge a cook by their knives. If they were dull, then it was going to be bad meal. This was actually one point on which Mom and I agreed. I had years of practice in her kitchen, working as her sous chef for most of my childhood, so slicing came easily to me. I used to hate the monotony of slicing, but Mom used these menial chores to train and prepare me to be a Vietnamese bride. She knew I could learn to meet the *Công*, be skillful, one of those four virtues required of a woman.

I made the sauce and tasted it a few times to be sure it was just right. I usually cook without any recipes so tasting is vital to pulling off a great dish. I was careful to use a new spoon to taste each time to keep everything clean. I didn't want to be caught on camera double-dipping. That would really be embarrassing. Mom would no doubt have disowned me and publicly denied I was her daughter, even though in our culture double-dipping was considered quite normal.

I deep-fried my thinly sliced shallots and placed them on napkins to soak up the excess oil. I could hear the commotion my competitors were making all around me but mostly ignored everything except the work in front of me. One exception was the familiar aroma of curry, which I had to pause to savor, ever so briefly. My favorite Indian chef was cooking up some amazing flavors two stations away from me. She looked beautiful today in a green sari with silver trim. Peter, always skilled at catching you unawares, sidled up to me and broke my concentration.

"Kieu, what are you making?" he asked.

"I'm preparing my mom's own recipe of Vietnamese Feminine Salad."

"Why do you think you're going to win *Sliced and Diced*?" he asked point-blank.

No time to stall. No time to think. All I could do was sound confident.

"Because I'm the best cook here!" I replied, smiling, as if his question was almost too obvious to deserve a reply. My tone was rushed, with a teaspoon of annoyance and a pinch of hidden pride. I was sure the producers would love it – but would my fellow contestants hate me for it?

My sharp competitive nature developed when I was introduced to tennis. It was a bourgeois sport for Vietnamese, played by generations of men in my family. I still have old black-and-white photos of my great-grandfather standing in his black pants and white shirt and shoes holding a tennis racket in his hands. The French brought this gift to our people. It was a modern and gentlemanly sport of the upper classes.

I was living in Paris in 1984 when our step-uncle gave my brother Minh and I lessons. I loved playing tennis because it was one time I was allowed to run around in the sun. I didn't have much of a forehand, but as Step-Uncle liked to say, my backhand was as dependable as a cobra strike. He gave me pats on the head and bravos whenever I lashed a backhand winner. Some might think of tennis as stuffy and tradition-bound, but for me, it was pure fun to be out there, away from the constraints of disapproving eyes and cultural rules and etiquette, free at last to move my body as much as I wanted.

One day in the middle of a tennis lesson I felt a strange, sharp pain somewhere near my stomach. I excused myself to go to the bathroom, but sitting there I grew even more frustrated. Nothing was happening. But the intense cramps persisted. The pain was so blinding, I finally had to ask Step-Uncle to take us home. He knew I was not a complainer and was very concerned that something serious must be wrong. He rushed us to the Metro to bring me back to Mom's apartment. The ride could not have lasted more than fifteen minutes, but to this day I would swear it must have taken hours. I sat in my seat bent over at the waist and squirmed around to try to ease the pain, but nothing helped. I had never experienced anything like that agony and was sure I would end up in the hospital. I was so relieved to see Mom's face when she opened the door.

"What happened?" she asked.

"I don't know, my stomach hurts," I replied while rushing into my bedroom to lie down. I just wanted the pain to end.

Mom came into my bedroom a few minutes later with something in her hand.

"Put this on," she said, handing it to me.

I looked down and recognized the object as something I had often seen in our bathroom: a feminine pad.

"What do you mean put it on?" I asked her.

She opened the plastic wrap, removed the pad from the wrapper, and removed the tape to reveal the sticky side.

"Stick this on your underwear."

I got up and went to the bathroom and followed her instructions. Soon I had a pillow between my legs. I didn't understand why. But I hoped it might somehow help my stomach pain. I went back to the bedroom to crawl into my bed.

"Rest here," my mother said and left the room.

After a while the waves of pain eased and I decided to go to the bathroom. I held up the pad, not believing what I was seeing: It was soaked red with blood. I was horrified. I had no idea what was happening but had the sense to replace the bloodied pad with another one. Mom had not seemed overly concerned, so it seemed unlikely I was going to die.

My cramps eventually went away, but I continued to wear the pads daily for the next two months. I had heard in passing about women bleeding when they get older and did not want to be unprepared the next time it happened. I came home from school one day and Mom called me into her bedroom. What did I do now? I thought.

"Why are you still wearing those pads?" she asked firmly.

She had grown concerned seeing used pads in the little trash can in the bathroom day after day.

"Because of the bleeding," I replied, standing meekly in her doorway.

I was upset. I did not like discussing my private affairs with her. Mom looked a little shocked.

"But you're not bleeding anymore," she said.

"I don't know when it will happen again," I said, "so I wear it just in case."

She sighed and seemed relieved. In fact, she chuckled.

"You only bleed once a month for a week and at the same time each month," Mom informed me.

Now she tells me!

"I did not know."

I was so happy to find out that I did not have to wear those darn pillows every day for the rest of my life. Before I was allowed to go back to my room Mom warned me to remember that I was a girl and I was never allowed to wear tampons. I had seen those things in the bathroom, too, and was curious about them, but mostly I was grateful she answered that question so I didn't have to ask. That was Mom. No explanation, just statements of fact.

The topic of sex was never discussed in my family. We were told babies came from armpits. I suppose it was just as ridiculous as stories about storks delivering babies to American homes. To this day I don't even know the word for sex in Vietnamese. They usually referred to sex as *làm bậy bạ* (doing the naughty) when referring to the act in bad scenarios. In happy, loving situations, they said *chăn gối vợ chồng* (blankets pillows wife husband). I did appreciate the subtleties of the Vietnamese culture when referring to sex. It was never crude or lewd.

"Five, four, three, two, ONE!" Peter called out happily. "Time is up!"

We all had to raise our hands in the air to demonstrate we had stopped at the sound of Peter shouting at us. I was amazed that one hour could pass so quickly. I looked down at my beautiful Feminine Salad. I had plated an array of colorful, perfectly julienned vegetables and herbs on a large white platter. I carefully placed the fried shallots in the center, and added chopped peanuts and a sprig of cilantro. The extra dipping sauce was ready for the judges to pour over the salad before they tasted it. I knew even Mom would be proud. I pulled off all four virtues today. I was skillful. I was cute. I was articulate. And I played nice.

One by one they ushered each of us into a separate room to give our presentation in front of the judges and an array of cameras. I sat waiting on the couch next to Todd, a porky, middle-age contestant with the ruddy complexion of someone who had been overweight most of his life. As much as I hated chit-chat, I forced myself to save my nerves by letting Todd talk. I found out he was a father of two. He tried out for the show to remind his kids they could do anything they wanted. He loved bacon. He didn't even have to tell me this. I could tell just by looking at him that he was a fan of bacon and Southern comfort food. But his energy and demeanor did help calm me down. That would benefit me in front of the judges.

"Who doesn't love bacon?" I told Todd, smiling.

Vietnamese people tended to rely on intuition. We developed this skill as a necessity because we were not able to ask questions. Reading a person's mood and body language offered us clues into their thoughts and character. I was very good at reading people's energies and making sure they could not read mine, practicing a steady and natural self-control. Americans often lacked this level of awareness. They didn't bother. It was perfectly natural for me to meet a complete stranger and after three and a half minutes they had revealed their entire dating history to me. It was much different with my Vietnamese friends. We could spend a whole weekend to-gether on a camping trip, cooking, eating and laughing together, yet head back home afterward having directly shared very little about each other. Perhaps each other's professions and maybe marital sta-tus, but that was about it. But we could clue into where each person came from by judging their accent. We could determine the family's education level by their choice of words and their mannerisms as they ate. We could gauge their honesty by the way they glanced at us. Looking into another person's eyes too long as they spoke would be considered too intimate. The practice of looking just long enough to show interest followed by a timely release was an art form, one I knew I would need to practice to perfection during the shooting for *Sliced and Diced*.

Packing for the trip to New York had been horrendous. I stuffed as many clothes, shoes and accessories as I could into three suitcases, knowing I might be gone as long as three months and wishing I could pack three or four more suitcases. John had a strange look in his eye as he stood back and watched me bounce around from closet to closet and drawer to drawer to gather my things. I could never understand how he was able to pack in less than an hour and have everything he needed while I made lists and checked them twice yet always ended up borrowing something from his suitcase. But then there was a lot about John I could never understand. He had his good qualities, like discretion; he knew enough to stay out of the way to avoid becoming a victim of my anxiety as I rushed around. As calm as he appeared, his excitement for me came through, along with something harder to put my finger on, an uneasiness he tried to camouflage. I had to wonder: Would he prefer to have the woman he married years ago, less sure of herself, more afraid of the world, or the changed woman who would come home to him after appearing on *Sliced and Diced*? Maybe none of that really mattered so long as I did come home to him.

Unlike in the car on the drive down to L.A., when I wanted to talk and he clung to his audio-book safety blanket, here at home he seemed to want to open the lines of communication between us, not in any deep way, but at least enough to lessen the sense that we were two trains heading away from each other in the night. This time I was the one who did not want to be distracted. I had to make good decisions about clothes and I had to stay focused on positive thinking. I was not even going to consider the possibility that I might fall short and be eliminated from the show in the early going. I was going to get as much air time as possible and do my best to land my own cooking show. To pull that off I'd have to be determined and I'd have to be smart. That meant backing off on black. I was only going to bring two black dresses, even though black is my favorite color because it camouflages my back fat and belly pooch. But for *Sliced and Diced* I had to go in a different direction. Bright, flashy color, that was what they wanted. A colorful personality and a colorful wardrobe, this was the winning combination.

I packed my back-fat-suppressing Soma bras and Spanx undergarments. After turning thirty-five, I found my fat migrating from one spot on my body to another on a weekly basis. I felt lucky not to have big thighs, but hated my stomach pooch. I had two bellies, one for eating food and the other for storing food. I'd had them since I was thirteen, even when I was just a dark, short twig with breasts. A few years back I finally learned to accept them after attending a seminar in San Francisco about women and body image. During one of the sessions, they made us stand half-naked in front of a mirror. Staring into those long, flimsy wardrobe mirrors, we had to pretend that the body parts we hated most had voices. We had conversations with them. I had paid six hundred bucks for this woo-woo seminar, so I reluctantly went through the exercise. I studied the reflection of my 115-pound, five-foot-one body, in a pair of black short shorts and white tank top. I rolled up the shirt to expose the body parts I liked least.

"Hey twins, why can't one of you leave?" I taunted my belly rolls. "I only need one. You're so flabby and fat!"

The coach was standing next to me and loved this. He coaxed me along, but I felt silly and could not help chuckling.

"What would your bellies say back to you?" the coach asked me in a way-too-serious tone of voice.

I was going to chuckle some more, I felt the laughter coming, but suddenly it hit me: He was right. This was the way. I stared back into the mirror with fury and purpose and could hear a voice in my head now.

"Why do you speak to us this way?" I shouted, channeling the voice of my twin bellies. "Would you allow anyone else to call us names like that?"

I was startled by the intensity of the outburst.

"No, I wouldn't," I said after a pause. "Even my husband knows never to call me names."

The women who had gathered around me started sobbing. My words cut right through the fog and made them stop and take stock. We get offended when others speak degradingly to us. Yet we do it to ourselves every single day of our lives.

In that moment I learned something wonderful. I gave myself permission to love my body for the first time, despite its flaws. I gathered up all the name-calling and criticism I received growing up about my weight, height and skin tone and stuffed it all away in a little bag. I vowed that day I would no longer call my belly my "twins" and never have. I would stop complaining about them. I would love them. Because they are me. I have not seen that bag since.

Jessica, an attractive woman in cat-eye glasses and Louboutin heels, walked confidently back into the room after completing her presentation and flashed a coy smile. She had dark brown shoulder-length hair in a blunt cut with short bangs. Her shtick was making daily food elegant.

"Kieu, you're next!" she called out, all but winking.

I grabbed my platter and held it up high as I walked in to meet the judges, giving them my best confident smile.

"Hi, Kieu!" said the oldest of the judges, who was thin and distinguished-looking, like a real judge. "Welcome to your first official on-camera presentation."

Sitting to his left was Peter. On his right was a redheaded woman with wavy hair, a distracted air and a smile plastered on her face that looked permanent.

"Kieu, you remember our judges?" Peter spoke up in his official tone. "Gnarles, our executive producer, and Linda, our head chef. And I am your third judge."

"Hello judges," I said firmly but evenly. "Thank you for this opportunity."

"You have three minutes to present your dish on camera," Peter stated matter-of-factly. "And we will taste your dish to determine if you will be sliced today. Are you ready?"

The director immediately said "Cut!"

A makeup artist came running out to powder my nose. The director reworked the camera angle and gave multiple instructions to the room full of people.

"Action!" the director finally shouted after ten minutes of commotion.

I smiled at the camera once again and gave them a presentation I knew they would not forget.

"Hi, my name is Kieu," I said. "I'm going to show you how to make Vietnamese food easy by using American ingredients."

I took a breath and continued to smile confidently at the camera. Twice I realized my eyes had darted from the judges to the blinking light on top of the camera and back, but I was not going to let nervousness upset my composure. Steady, steady, steady.

"Today I made for you Vietnamese Feminine Salad," I continued. "This salad represents all that is intricate and beautiful about women. It has amazing textures of crunchy vegetable and fried sweet potato and soft herbs. The taste is well balanced with sweet, sour and salt."

I had found a groove. I could feel warm waves of approval emanating from the judges.

"All you have to do is pour on this delicious dressing of lime juice, a little sugar, and some fish sauce to give it that *VietnamEazy* flavor,"

I said.

I demonstrated by pouring the sauce over the platter, holding my elbow high to give the gesture some added flair.

"Toss it a little and serve it tableside," I added.

I picked up a small plate from under the counter and set it down. I tossed the salad with two large, metal spoons and served a little portion onto the plate. Holding up the plate with one hand and chopsticks in the other, I tasted a small bite – and was honestly surprised at how delicious and perfect the dish had turned out.

"Mmmmmm, it's so good, with a fresh crunch, like having summer in your mouth," I said, flashing honest pride.

I put the plate and chopsticks down and turned to look directly at the camera, a twinkle in my eyes, and added, "The next time you think Vietnamese food is hard? Think easy. I'm Kieu and I look forward to making your next culinary adventure *VietnamEazy*."

We all had to wait in a plain small room with a few simple couches until all the contestants had their turn at presenting their dishes. The last person to go up was Deepti, my favorite Indian chef. She had a mild and gentle demeanor about her that I admired. She was full of light and smiles. I wished I could watch her presentation and was sure I could pick up a few pointers from her approach. But you never really knew on these shows what the judges would consider bad or consider great. I had seen the worst chefs win and the greatest ones lose. That was probably part of the calculation to keep the regular viewer at home interested. Still, talent and grace had to count for something and if I did not win the competition, I hoped that Deepti would. She had made Lamb Keema Aloo, minced lamb curry with potato and basmati rice, and the dish looked exquisite.

I was exhausted from having to wait but kept myself entertained by studying the other contestants' body language, looking for insights into their personalities. Some slumped on the sofa in a defeated state. Some paced back and forth. Some chatted nonstop. Still others sat still, pulled back into themselves, and engaged in some private dialogue about how they could improve in the next round – if they made it that far. Suddenly the door flew open and Peter pranced in.

"The judges would like to see Todd, Jessica and ..." he said.

The rest of us all stared down. It seemed like forever before he continued.

"And ... Deepti!"

I'd been on pins and needles waiting to hear my name, but once the moment had passed it dawned on me that maybe I was lucky not to have been named. Todd, Jessica and Deepti followed Peter out of the room, looking like characters in *The Hunger Games*. Deepti glanced back to meet my eye and I nodded and smiled as if to say, "You'll be OK." She smiled her thanks but then quickly turned back around to adjust her sari and straighten her posture into a dignified stance before following Peter out of the room.

Chatter exploded all around me once the door shut behind them. It felt as if the air had left the room. To make up for the lack of oxygen, everyone speculated even more rapidly on whether or not the departed trio represented the top three, the bottom three or some as-yet-unimaginable other three. My own guess was that if Deepti were part of the group, they had to be the top three, just based on the wonderful fragrances wafting my way from her kitchen, but I was also thrown off because then what would Todd be doing in that group? The bacon guy? He just did not seem like a star to me, but I had been wrong before. Who knew how far the producers would go to try to satisfy viewers? The Vietnamese woman and the sari-wearing Indian woman were not necessarily going to make your average middle-American viewer feel comfortable, were we? I made a mental note to talk to Deepti later about clothes if she did return to the competition.

We had no idea what to expect when after twenty minutes the door swung open and the three of them filed back in among us. Todd was grinning from ear to ear and finally blurted out, "I'm the winner!"

Jessica and Deepti were beaming, too, while we all clapped for

Todd and congratulated him. He kept looking down bashfully, as if he had never won anything in his life and could not believe he had now.

"And," he said, smiling so much he had to stop and start again, "I have immunity for the next round."

Cue up another hearty round of applause and congratulations. Todd let that play out, still looking down modestly, then sharply inhaled, like a chain-smoker finishing off a butt.

"And the judges would like to see Helen, Taylor and … Luke," he added solemnly.

The rest of us were so relieved, we could not begin to hide our true feelings. Which brought me back to Todd. I could see it now: He was an actor! I would forever be shocked that any dish he prepared could possibly win out over Deepti's amazing curry, but we all knew part of the show was performance and self-packaging. Clearly, Todd had hidden talents in this area. He was a chameleon. He could hit any note he wanted. Within fifteen seconds he could rearrange his emotions from exhilarated to humble to apologetic and back again. He might not have the moves in the kitchen, but he had been placed on the show by his agent and there was no denying he could win the whole thing if someone did not take him out. I would have to plan my strategy against him very carefully. He might look like a lightweight, but he was deceptively clever. It was shrewd of him to start with a dish of shrimp and grits with bacon and tomatoes. Even curry, a dish packed with flavor, simply cannot compete against bacon. A meek dish like mine, Feminine Salad, had no shot at all, no matter how fine and exquisite and delicately balanced it might have been. My approach to the next round was going to take this idea and run with it. I would see his bacon and raise it! My dish would be big and bold, tasty and tantalizing. To beat bacon, I would go deep fried!

3

In the Time of the Emperor

>≡≡><

VEGETARIAN IMPERIAL ROLLS
Nem or Chả Giò Chay

In Vietnam, vegan dishes are usually served during Buddhist ceremonies, so the egg contained in the Chinese wrappers – giving rise to the name "egg rolls" – would not be allowed. Rice paper is commonly used as the wrapper for these deep-fried rolls. It is more delicate and more difficult to work with, so most restaurants in America take a shortcut by using the sturdier Chinese egg roll shells. But once you've had Vietnamese Imperial Rolls fried with rice paper, you will never want the egg roll version again.

6 Servings

INGREDIENTS:

1 package of dry rice paper shells
Olive oil
Oil for frying

(Continued on next page)

Filling:

1 carrot
1 block firm tofu
10 white mushrooms
1/2 pound taro
1 teaspoon sugar
4 teaspoons soy sauce
4 teaspoons ground black pepper

Dipping Sauce:

1 1/2 teaspoons sugar
2 teaspoons soy sauce
2 teaspoons hot water
1 Thai chili (optional)

Garnish:

1 head lettuce, leaves separated, washed and dried
1 bunch cilantro, stems cut off, washed and dried
1 bunch mint, stems cut off, washed and dried

Mix all the dipping sauce ingredients in bowl. Add hot sauce or chopped chili if desired. Set aside.

For the filling, julienne carrot, tofu, mushrooms and taro into thin strips an Inch or two long. Set aside. Heat up a pot of oil. Deep fry the tofu and taro for three minutes. Remove and drain on paper towel.

Heat 4 teaspoons of olive oil in a pan, then add the raw vegetables and deep-fried tofu and taro. Stir for four minutes.

Assembly: Fill a large shallow bowl with warm water. Find a hard even surface (wood block or large plate) to work on. Remove one rice paper at a time, quickly dip it in warm water and place on wood block. Scoop 1 to 2 teaspoons of filling and place in the center of rice paper. With your fingers, gently shape filling into a long shape. Fold in the two sides over the filling, then gently roll up the wrapper like a burrito. Do not overfill or wrap too tightly as the filling will expand during cooking and the rice paper may break. Place wrapped rolls on a plate, being sure to keep them well separated so they don't stick together.

In a deep pot, heat up oil to 350 degrees. Add a few rolls at a time and cook for five minutes or until golden brown. Do not turn rolls over too many times or they will break. Do not put too many in the oil as this will cause the oil temperature to drop. Frying anything in oil that is not hot enough will render soggy rolls. Place fried rolls on paper towel to soak up excess oil.

To serve the rolls, place them on a large platter with lettuce, cilantro and mint on the side. Serve with the dipping sauce on the side. Enjoy these delicate rolls by wrapping them inside a lettuce leaf with cilantro and mint, and dip in sauce.

I spent about a millisecond feeling good that it was Luke and Taylor who were eliminated in the first round and not me. I let myself enjoy the odd mixture of thrill and relief that came with knowing I was alive in the competition. But I also knew the clock was ticking. As soon as the show was aired on TV, my mother would be wound up full of tips, unwanted advice and reprimands. "You got lucky!" she would blurt out at me over the phone in Vietnamese, or she would just think the thought so loudly, I would feel it in my bones. "You could have been knocked out! Really you lost that round. Do you want me to tell you why?"

My answer, if I gave one, would of course be, "No, Mom, that's the last thing I want," but it did not matter if I spoke or did not speak, sighed or did not sigh. The question was rhetorical and I was going to get an earful from her. Even without picking up the phone, I could hear a stream of critical words from her, the consonants all running together. I didn't want to think about that now. I wanted to fill myself with happy, empowering thoughts. I let myself float back into the past to remember times when I was happy. When Ngoại was happy. When she cheerfully and proudly recounted the stories of her father and how they lived. I loved her stories. To me they were Vietnamese fairy tales of beautiful days gone by, days I would never know and only dreamed of from time to time. Those were imperial days of her childhood where she grew up in wealth, opulence, comfort and laughter. Life outside of Vietnam was not easy for us so she liked to tell us stories of her childhood to ease the financial hardship that fell upon her during the prime of her life.

Ngoại was born a middle child to a family of six children in Hanoi. Her father, Papa, studied to be a physician at the University of Indochina in Hanoi. He knew French, played tennis and was quite a ladies' man. Ngoại and Mom inherited his high-bridge nose and light-toned skin. He did not complete medical school as he changed his course of study halfway through because of his dislike of blood. He managed to finish his university law degree and dutifully got married immediately. He easily secured a post as the mayor of a small village outside of Hanoi with his university degree and family wealth.

He loved being a mayor because he was able to offer hands-on help to the people in his village. Every evening before dinner, he rode out to visit the town's people on his brown horse, followed by two of his guards on foot. He wore the traditional imperial *áo dài* tailored for men. People would bow to him to show him respect as he rode by.

I was jolted out of my early morning daydream haze when Peter walked into the bedroom I shared with three other female contestants. He flicked on the lights and surprised all of us. It was 5 a.m. and still pitch dark outside. We were in our pajamas, uncoiffed hair and not a speck of makeup. I hated to imagine how I would look once this episode aired on TV. I sat up, covering my body with the pink blanket and clutching it as if it were a binky.

"Get up, everyone!" said Peter cheerfully. "We are going on a road trip! Get dressed and meet me downstairs in fifteen minutes."

He had this way of finishing all his sentences with a singsong quality. Then he turned around to slide out of the room as the two cameramen followed. I caught the eye of one of them lingering a little too long in the vicinity of my chest. How annoying was that? It did not bother me that the cameras saw us in skimpy clothing, but I hated to be woken up in a startled state. When this happens, my heart goes racing and my anxiety kicks into high gear.

My thoughts scrolled to all the past episodes of *Sliced and Diced* to do a quick comparison to figure out what the surprise would be. It could be anything. Maybe we would have to cook with our bare hands and no utensils or, worse yet, be part of a team competition. I like people well enough, but I have to work double-time to be politically correct, hold back on barking orders, allow others to chime in. In other words, it would be an exhausting experience.

We all got dressed as quickly as we could. I grabbed my makeup bag and threw it in my tote along with my flat shoes. I figured I could do my face during the torturous ride in the car. I would have to figure out how I could ride in the front to avoid getting sick. Did other people wake up with their minds racing a mile a minute like mine? I always wondered about that. Probably not.

I started to see a doctor a few years back just to see what counseling was all about. During my first session, I explained to him that I experienced sweaty armpits whenever I got on the phone. To my surprise, he said this was not normal. He said it was a symptom of anxiety. I absorbed the information, refused to label myself as he did, and easily masked my symptoms with a clear deodorant stick to skip the mood-altering drugs.

It was not acceptable for us Vietnamese to have mood disorders. It was not allowed. We labeled these people crazy or weak. I remember we had a cousin who was mentally unstable and he would self-medicate with drugs. He sometimes acted a little nuts around us and Ngoại would whisper under her breath to us that he was crazy and that we should stay away from him. During one of his visits, he looked into the mirror in our living room and said, "There's a man looking back at me, make him go away." Minh and I looked at each other and burst out laughing. Ngoại gave us disapproving looks and turned to him with her Northern Vietnamese smile while she completely ignored his question and offered him more tea.

There were many clear distinctions among Northerners and Southerners. One important distinction was that Northerners were pretentious and Southerners were blunt. Neither trusted the other. It was not uncommon to ask someone you just met where their family came from so you could immediately classify whether you could trust them or not.

My veins were pumped with a mix of Northern and Central Vietnamese blood, yet I was raised in the South. My accent is a mix of Southern and Northern. At home, I only heard the accents of the educated class in Hanoi. At school, I adopted a Southern accent of Saigon. Grandma was grateful I was not raised by my father or his family. They came from Central Vietnam and their accents were considered country, or the American equivalent of hick. Even I could not tell if I would be classified as trustworthy or not based on these rules. Were there exceptions for people like me?

I hopped on the large touring bus with the huge *Sliced and Diced* logo and a photo of Peter plastered on the side panel. I grabbed the first open seat I could find and wished I had taken my Dramamine. Bus rides were even worse than car rides. Across the aisle next to me was Miranda, who was tall and slender to a fault. A shaft of sunlight was shining on her in a way that made her light blonde hair glow. I had a momentary thought that she could be an angel, but the spell was obliterated when she spoke.

"Oh, boy, I hope we get to make desserts today," she said in a high-pitched, nasal tone that reminded me of screeching cats. "I'm dying for some cupcakes!"

She was my roommate. I liked her well enough, but could not stand that voice.

"I hope not," was my short reply.

I worried my irritation might be showing, so I tried to soften my comment.

"You're so great at making desserts." It was the best I could come up with so early in the morning.

Miranda's show was about cupcakes. She could make everything into a cupcake, even roast chicken or pesto sauce.

All the contestants were finally on the bus and the director also piled in. As soon as all the cameras were in position, Peter made his grand entrance.

"Good morning, everyone!" he cried out.

Then his voice dropped an octave and he turned serious.

"There are ten of you left, and one of you will be eliminated today. Todd, congratulations, you have immunity for this round."

The second cameraman zoomed in to Todd's grinning face.

"We are going on a wonderful ride today around Manhattan!"

Everyone cheered and clapped and I thought to myself how I loved Manhattan. I spent a month there with a boyfriend once when I was very young, too young to realize it would never last. Magical moments shared with another human being were rare for me; my guard was always up. I could count on one hand the moments in the first thirty-eight years of my life when I allowed myself to be loved, accepted love, and did not ask for anything in return. Sometimes, I wondered if it ever happened at all. As the years passed, those memories faded into edited snapshots of moments of happiness.

The skill to draw up an invisible shield around me on command came not only from my personal misfortune, but also as a result of the Communist takeover of Vietnam. Once the Viet Cong seized Saigon, I remember being taught to tell white lies in order to protect ourselves from being arrested. An example of a lie Ngoại taught me was, "If you ever get stopped by the Viet Cong police and they ask you what you ate at home, never, ever tell them meat. You have to always say vegetables."

I was confused by her instructions because we were always taught that kids should never lie, that lying was bad and we should mirror Grandma's impeccable record of truth. She saw the surprise on my face and explained with worry and seriousness in her eyes.

"The Viet Cong have changed everything about our lives, and you must now learn to do this so we can stay alive," she said. "Do you understand?"

"Yes, Ngoại." Her calm tone and concerned eyes told me everything. I did not need to ask any more questions.

One of the ultimate improprieties in behavior from a conscious adult was to pry information out of children. Innocence was to be encouraged, cherished and prolonged as long as possible. Life and all its sufferings would take it away soon enough.

To live among the Viet Cong was to learn to display a totally different set of behaviors and values than we were used to. I was often stopped on my way to and from school by men in uniform asking me random questions about my home life. I remember the dark green uniforms, red bandanas around their arms, the yellow star they wore and the large guns they carried. They usually offered me and my brother a piece of candy to buy our trust and said the candy was from Bác Hồ, Uncle Ho Chi Minh. But we were taught well and never accepted their gifts. We shuffled our little feet ahead toward our destination as fast as we could without eye contact and remained quiet until we were bullied into giving them an answer. Years later, these rules were still playing out, even if American tourists were oblivious to them. Dislike for the upper class ran deep and those of us who survived did so only by learning to shift and play by their rules. I understood that everyone had a drive for survival. They had the right, the courage and the will to climb out of the hole of poverty to claim their spot in the sun. But that did not mean I could condone the continuous ruthless treatment of our people. Sometimes the ends simply did not justify the means.

Peter waited until the cheers died down and continued.

"Once we stop, you will have fifteen minutes and fifty dollars to purchase your ingredients and one hour to make a one-bite dish that will blow the judges away," he said.

The excitement bubbled within me as I thought "Yes! I can definitely make my grandma's Vegetarian Imperial Rolls." I can make a miniature version of them. Like the ones I had as a kid. They'll be fried and will beat Todd's bacon anything. Peter climbed off the bus and we saw him hop into his limo. I was invigorated and happy again and suddenly realized my lips had slipped into a smile.

One of Ngoại's favorite stories was how her father became a hero. She began the story with, "Your great-grandfather (*có oai và phong độ lắm*) was full of nobility and charisma." Her eyes would take on a faraway look as if she could see Papa standing right in front of her. There was an immediacy to her voice, as if he were there listening as she continued with her story of how he became admired and loved by all who knew him.

Papa heard a woman scream for help from one of the small houses and he quickly rode his horse toward the calls, leaving his guards on foot chasing behind him. As he approached the screaming sounds, he spotted a woman wearing a black cotton *đồ bộ*, similar to men's pajamas in style and worn by peasants. She frantically waved her hands in the air. He quickly stopped his horse and came to her side. She was about fifty years old with jet black teeth. In those days, aging gracefully did not encumber anyone's consciousness after the age of fifty; a village woman was simply happy to have all her teeth. She might as well have been one hundred for she looked it, even though her hair had only a thin streak of gray on the right side of her temple. Her black teeth had not become black naturally. They became black as a result of daily chewing of betel leaves with slivers

of areca palm nut and a bit of lime paste. It was a great way to pre-
serve teeth by preventing tooth decay, but the juice also turned white
teeth into a glistening black. This look became fashionable among
older women in the North.

The woman frantically told him what happened. It was hard to
make out what she was saying through her wailing and crying, but
he could pick out enough words to understand her troubles. Her
daughter-in-law had been in labor for hours yet the baby wouldn't
come and she was afraid something terrible would happen. Papa
quickly rolled up his sleeves, ran into the house and started to help
with delivering the baby. At the same time, one of his guards hopped
on his horse to go fetch the doctor who lived on the other side of
town. Thank goodness for Papa's short time spent in medical school
– he had an idea of what to do. His distaste for blood was overwhelmed by the need to save the poor young woman and her un-
born baby. By the time the doctor arrived, Papa had delivered the
baby. The doctor then took over, but from that point on Papa was
the hero of the village. Through time, the tale of the delivery grew
more and more elaborate and exaggerated and he became a legend
in our family as the greatest mayor of his day.

The bus sped up to make a stop light, executed a few quick turns,
and the next thing I knew we were in the middle of Little Italy
during the Feast of San Gennaro, the huge annual festival. Maybe
the driver was just stopping to ask for directions? Please! But no. The
big doors hissed open. Time for full-on panic. Italian? No, please,
anything but Italian. How was I going to make imperial rolls with
pasta and prosciutto? Time for Plan B. Only one problem: I had
no Plan B! I had been daydreaming the whole ride! A column of
frenzied ants began crawling up my spine toward the base of my
head. The anxiety was kicking into high gear. I prayed the hives

would not continue to spread and make a grand entrance on my face. Keep breathing, Kieu. Stay calm. I knew I would find a way to recover from this horrible twist. I could make *VietnamEazy* Spaghetti! Italian pasta recipes sometimes call for anchovies to boost richness – umami, as the foodies call it. Mom always added fish sauce to her spaghetti meat sauce. I often snuck a little in at home without telling my husband and smiled graciously as I accepted his rave review.

I started the whole *VietnamEazy* concept because of my husband. His disdain for the strong smell of fish sauce often led me to substitute salt to satisfy his taste. But the trick with cooking fish sauce was to simmer it long enough to reach the point of indescribable delicacy where the pungent smell is replaced by a sweet, savory umami aroma. This essence is unique to Southeast Asian cuisines.

We lined up against the bus in single file and waited for Peter to get out of his limo. Then we waited as he walked toward us and twice had to stop so his makeup artist, hustling along at his side, could reach out with a brush to make last-minute adjustments to his face. She was one talented artist.

"OK, everyone," Peter said in that same playful deadpan voice he always used for the show. "We are now going to take a little walk. Follow me."

He motioned us to trail him like schoolchildren on a day trip. I looked around at this huge city full of hustle and bustle. There were young men and women sitting at tables lined up outside cafes and restaurants having their simple breakfast. I could smell the aroma of roasted coffee and the musical sound of the Italian language. Everyone stared at our convoy. To my amazement, we crossed the street and stopped in front of a huge, red Asian Supermarket sign. Peter turned around and was all giddy, like a child who successfully surprised an adult.

"Welcome to Chinatown!" he called out with a grin.

"You are going into this wonderful Asian market to gather your ingredients." I heard some cheers and oh-my-gods coming from the contestants. A few of them glared at me as if I had personally arranged the Chinatown visit. Jessica was among them. She realized I saw her and now had to say something to me to recover.

"Well, Kieu, this is your lucky day, isn't it?" she asked, her jealousy not at all well concealed.

"Welcome to my world!" I replied. It was a little cheeky, but I couldn't help myself.

Anyway, what was the big deal? Chinese food was hardly foreign to Americans. It was no more foreign than Italian or Mexican. You could get sweet and sour, moo goo gai pan, beef broccoli and egg foo yung all day long. These were all "ChinEazy" dishes, Chinese food made easy for Americans. I listened as Jessica continued on and on about her upbringing and how lavish her lifestyle was, a clear signal of her unease in such a "filthy" neighborhood. Her clothes were perfectly tailored to fit her lean, size-six frame. Her feet were like Cinderella's, fine and dainty. I know this because only thin feet were made to fit in Christian Louboutin red sole heels. For those of us who had wider feet, these shoes would make our toes bleed within five minutes. You always found her standing in them no matter what circumstance we were in. To the untrained eye, you would immediately know money was not something she lacked. But there was more to her story. The way she laughed gave her away.

You could tell a lot about a woman by the way she laughed. At least, a Northern girl could. Northern girls are thoroughly trained in how we carry ourselves, including the way we laugh. A proper laugh signified your family rank and status in society. First, we cover our mouth to conceal our teeth. Second, the laughter has to be contained and not too loud. Third, the sound must have the appropriate coyness, with throaty girlish notes. Finally, the sound can only last for a few seconds. Laughter from deep within our gut accompanied by an uncovered, open mouth was appalling. Gut-bursting laughter was rare and never acceptable in public or even at home. I remember Ngoại scolding my aunts if they allowed their laughter to go on too long or were too loud.

"Girls should not laugh like that, it's unbecoming!" she would reprimand them. "Your behavior is like those who have torn underwear tight undershirt, swollen shoulders large biceps, fistful of unruly armpit hair, downing Chinese tea in one breath – *tụi khố rách áo ôm, vai u thịt bắp mồ hôi dầu, lông nách một nạm, trà Tàu một hơi.*" This phrase always made me laugh because it painted a picture of a beefy, bald, sweaty man with long armpit hair, holding a small tea cup downing it as if it were a tequila shot. Ngoại and Mom often used this phrase to refer to Viet Cong soldiers who came from farmer stock and had no class.

I felt right at home running around the Chinese market. I had no problems finding my ingredients as I watched my competition go down the American food aisle to gather ingredients they knew. The most difficult ingredient for me to find in an American market would have been taro. Substituting it with potato would alter the flavor and texture quite a bit, so I felt today was my lucky day. Maybe Jessica was right: I had to win this one.

"Kieu, how confident do you feel about this round?" Peter asked me suddenly.

I hadn't even seen him coming. This was my TV bitch moment. I had to take advantage of it fully to establish my Ruthless Asian Chick character. Even if I lost, the audience would remember my comment.

"Isn't it obvious, Peter?" I said, flashing an ice-cold smile. "No one will out-cook me in this round. It's mine to win!"

Then, motioning my index fingers down toward the ground for effect, I added, "I'm going to take them down!"

I even surprised myself! I revealed my innermost competitive zeal right on national TV. The words would either be played while

I triumphantly claimed my prize, or as comedic relief – and rebuke of the overconfident Asian girl – when I was eliminated, in which case the clip would end up on *The Soup*. Peter looked delighted to have bagged a controversial comment and you could almost see him making a note to himself to ask the producer for a raise before the next season started.

After we paid for our purchases, we jumped onto the bus once more to drive back to the studio to cook. I imagined the taste of the imperial rolls as I tried to improve the recipe by adding or removing a few things. No. I would not mess with tradition; these Vegetarian Imperial Rolls had to be authentic. There was no need for Dramamine on this bus ride. The warmth of the sun touched my face as I relaxed and felt the comfort of the bus seat enveloping my body.

The funniest story Ngoại told was about Papa's foot guards. He had two who were always with him as his bodyguards. They spent their days around him and took naps in the courtyard while the kids teased them. They lived with the family most of the year, but in separate quarters along with the help. The children's favorite guard was Khải. He was a funny man who played with them. He had a tobacco addiction. He smoked *thuốc lào* (tobacco) out of a bamboo pipe called *điếu cày* (farmer's pipe) after lunch to aid his digestion. The children were fascinated with the tedious process he had to go through just to light up. He first filled his pipe with a little water and pressed a small amount of tobacco into it. Then he lit the end of the pipe with a match and inhaled a few times to help the fire simmer into the tobacco to create an ember. He gently exhaled back into the pipe, making a gurgling sound. The children were fascinated by this and snuck around to watch him smoke and laughed when his eyes glazed over as he leaned back against a tree to enjoy his high and drift off to sleep, his pipe at his side. They covered their mouths to conceal their laughter as they watched.

One afternoon while Khải was sleeping, Ngoại's youngest brother, Tuân, went in the kitchen and scraped off some black char from the wood-burning cooking area with a stick. He crept up on the sleeping guard, whose slumber was so deep he was snoring with his mouth wide open. Tuân grabbed Khải's pipe, smeared black char all around the mouthpiece with his fingers, and snuck the pipe back gently next to the sleeping guard. After a while Khải made a loud snorting sound and woke himself up. He looked around and didn't see anyone so he picked up his tobacco pipe to smoke it again. He lit it and smoked it for a few minutes and fell back asleep. The children got bored watching him sleep so they moved on to other childhood games.

Upon waking up again, Khải went into the living area where everyone was gathered for their afternoon snack. Everyone looked up as he entered the room and burst out laughing uncontrollably. Even Papa was rolling with laughter while Maman tried to retain her dignified composure and laughed while covering her mouth with her right hand. Khải's mouth had a perfect black 'O' on it from the tar that was smeared on his pipe. He didn't have a clue why everyone was laughing and pointing at him. Maman rushed to grab her embroidered handkerchief, handed it to him, and made a motion with her hand for him to wipe his mouth. She wanted to help end his humiliation and pretended to scold the children. They grew up happy in a home of gentle discipline and sunny afternoons of laughter until one day the sun went away for Ngoại.

I knew I had to keep sad thoughts away from my head the day of this pivotal *Sliced and Diced* competition. I would dedicate this win to Ngoại, the grandmother, the woman who brought smiles and happiness into my life when my parents were not there to raise me. We arrived back at the studio where Peter signaled us to gather in the kitchen with our groceries in hand.

"Contestants!" he called out, raising his arm in the air with a flourish. "Go!"

I followed the recipe to perfection, the same recipe that had led to so many smiles and approving nods from friends. I washed the lettuce, mint leaves and cilantro and heated up the oil for deep frying. I used the mandolin grater to slice the vegetables, carefully avoiding shredding my own fingers in the process.

I saw Christian running around talking to himself. He was the funniest character among the contestants. He had a habit of addressing himself in the third person as if he had an invisible coach at all times. He opened the fridge and suddenly started talking in a strange Pee-wee Herman voice.

"Christian, why are you looking in here?" he asked himself. "You already bought everything you needed."

"Yeah, but I couldn't find the buttermilk. Where is the buttermilk?" he replied to himself, this time speaking in an almost normal voice, though he emphasized the T's and stretched out the ending of "butter" like Dana Carvey doing the Church Lady. A cameraman ran over to him as I thought to myself, "Attention whore!" Then I caught myself: Oh, yeah, I'd been making my own shameless bids for attention from those same cameras! I had to chuckle at myself, and that was the perfect thing to do. Laughing had a magical way of changing my mood, and I got back to concentrating on my dish.

When Ngoại was seven her mother, Maman, dressed her and Tuân in their finest. These clothes were specifically tailored for them using the latest patterns from France. The children were dressed in European styles, not the usual traditional street style of Vietnamese children. Tuân wore little navy shorts and a white-collared shirt. His hair was short and parted to the left and slicked back with his father's Brilliantine. He looked like an angel. Ngoại wore a white dress with ruffles and white socks and black patent leather shoes. She was happy to receive special attention from Maman while her sisters watched with envy.

Ngoại twirled in her dress and stole glances at her sisters to make sure they knew she was special. She always knew she was special. Her father sometimes took her – never her sisters – with him when he visited with the townspeople. He loved taking her to the only French restaurant in town to show her off. He'd order a steak frites. He would cut up little pieces of juicy steak for her while she ate the fries. She sat perfectly straight at the table and glanced around to make sure everyone watched her as she took each bite slowly. The villagers would congratulate and compliment their mayor for having such a beautiful daughter who looked just like him with light skin, big eyes and a high-bridge nose.

At the end of each meal, he would order a scoop of vanilla ice cream for her, served in a stainless steel cup and saucer. The creamy, sweet, velvety texture was her favorite. She felt the softness of the cream as it melted on her tongue and licked the spoon with great enthusiasm as he watched. This was their special time together.

But this day, Papa watched her with great pain in his eyes as he kneeled down in his bedroom and looked into his favorite's eyes and spoke softly, "You and Tuân are going on a visit with Tonton Phú and Tata Bạch Nga."

She wanted to know why they were going to see their aunt and uncle, but it wasn't polite for children to ask questions, so she just nodded. Maman took her time combing Ngoại's hair, put it in two braids and gently whispered to her to remember to be good and do as she was told. Ngoại wanted to know why no one else was going on this trip, but knew not to ask. Maman started to pack their clothes in two small suitcases. Papa said to leave it for the maid, but Maman only cried and said it was the last thing she would do for her children.

Ngoại recalled the look in Papa's eyes. She saw a great, unfathomable sadness in those eyes. Later she elaborated that she believed he must have hated his own weakness, but despite himself he could not go against his brother's wishes. These were customs he had to obey. When she spoke of him she was never angry. She knew he couldn't do anything more to keep her by his side. Maman picked up Ngoại and Tuân and held them tight, and she gave each of them a twenty-four karat gold necklace and a jade Buddha pendant to wear around their necks for protection, a tradition Ngoại kept with her own children and grandchildren. Ngoại and Tuân, age seven and five respectively, were taken away by their aunt and uncle. No explanation was ever given to the children.

Fathers were the head of the households, and if this figure was taken away by fate, then the oldest son would automatically gain authority over the family. Even his mother had to listen to him. Papa was the second oldest son and had no authority within the family. His older brother and wife were childless. After multiple miscarriages, they had given up hope of ever having their own children. Papa was blessed with seven children, four girls and three boys. He was given too much. Everyone believed he must have received all the good karma left to his parents by their ancestors and God did not leave any for his brother, which was why they had no children.

Papa's sister-in-law, Bạch Nga, had stern, cold eyes and soft, milky white skin. At the death of her father-in-law, her husband received all the inheritance and took the position as head of the family. Without children, her own position in the family, although only second below her mother-in-law, would never be respected. She had to produce children or she and her family would be forever scorned by her husband's family. Her personal happiness of having her own children was not her concern, but her family's honor had to be preserved. It was her duty to not shame her ancestors with her inability to produce children.

At the start, their arranged marriage was not fully supported by her mother-in-law. Bạch Nga's cheekbones were deemed too high. High cheekbones in Vietnamese women were not considered beautiful or revered as in Western society. High cheekbones on women were a "husband killing" (*sát chồng*) feature. This meant she would outlive her husband – one day her cheeks would cause him to die a young and, of course, tragic death.

She was accepted into the family only because her future husband begged his parents to pursue the marriage. He had only caught a single glimpse of her right arm and face on the street and fell in love with her translucent skin. Her pale white skin was her saving grace. Darker skin tones suggested one came from lowly farmer and peasant stock, whereas light skin tones were cherished as high-class, a symbol of wealth and education. She was married for nine years and was miserable with her inability to produce children. Instead of holding young babies in her arms to show her power, she wore numerous twenty-four karat gold bracelets, carved with dragons and phoenixes, from her wrists up to her elbows on both arms. Her only weapon of defense was wealth, for without it, the other family members would forget she held the second highest position of all the women in the home.

It was not unusual for extended family to adopt children from other family members. For example, for families who had ten children, the tenth child was usually seen as bad luck. It was not unusual to give this unlucky child to an aunt or a cousin to raise. Since Bạch Nga's sister-in-law had seven kids, it was only fair that she shared her children with her less fortunate sister-in-law. The two families lived far away, about one day of traveling time by train. Bạch Nga had only seen all the children once, but knew she wanted the two youngest as they would be able to adapt more readily to their new parents than the older children. She asked her husband to order his younger brother to share his last two children with them. She wanted a boy and a girl, so she could secure her place as head of the family. Papa was considered a man who was "weak of the spirit" with his family even though he was the mayor of a village. Duty and responsibility to his parents and brother were his first priority and he could not say no to his older brother. His wife hated him for it. She despised him for his inability to protect her children and for making her give them up. Being only the daughter-in-law, with no power in the family, she could not do anything about it. She could not kick or scream for she would disgrace her own family. It was her duty to obey her husband to avoid whispers from the neighbors and other family members. They had a wonderful marriage until the day her children were ripped away from her arms. It was the most disheartening moment of her life. She did not allow Papa in her bed after that day and barely spoke a few words to him for the rest of her life.

Girls were taught to hold their bitterness over unfair treatment deep inside. Even at weddings, the married couples were always reminded of this with the first sip of their Champagne as husband and wife. We all raised our glasses to toast and were told "the taste of Champagne represents the bitterness and spiciness of life. May you always face the bitter and spice of your marriage with courage." We all knew what marriage was and it was not for this Western notion of personal happiness and love. Marriage and children were a must and a duty in the heart of Vietnamese women.

Ngoại and Tuân were taken by the driver to their new home. They arrived in the early evening by car. It stopped in front of a big, maroon-colored wooden gate. Khải was their driver. He looked at the children with wet eyes and helped them get out of the car. He stood in front of the gate and knocked on the great door so loud that it startled Ngoại. A mousy maid with a long ponytail tied low at the nape of her neck opened the door and greeted them with a welcoming smile, which made Khải glad for the children. He had met their aunt and uncle before and did not have warm feelings toward them.

The maid motioned for them to come inside. Khải ran back to the car to get the two little wicker suitcases. Ngoại was in awe at how grand and empty the house was. There were no sounds of children or laughter. The only sounds she heard were their footsteps and leaves rustling in the wind as the evening set in. It was a traditionally built home with a brick courtyard with two tall trees in the middle. All the rooms faced the courtyard. The elaborately carved pillars and window panes were painted black. Aromas filled the air – pork belly grilled on charcoal, which she recognized as *Bún Chả*, and *Nem* (fried imperial rolls) served with thin vermicelli noodles and fresh mint. It must be what they would be having for their welcoming dinner.

She followed the maid toward the salon, or living room. She saw the figure of a tall woman pacing back and forth in the salon. It seemed she couldn't decide whether to sit or stand until she looked up and saw Ngoại and her brother. She straightened her posture and gazed directly at them. She wore a traditional dress of deep red velvet, *áo dài*, black long pants and gold bracelets on both wrists all the way up her elbows. She had so many on her lower arm it looked as if her arms were made of carved twenty-four karat gold. The bracelets made clanking sounds as she moved toward the children. She reached out to tap their shoulders lightly while smiling. It was her attempt to show them a little affection. Her husband stayed in his large carved wooden chair and smiled at the children as she herded them toward him to show him respect. They were both taught proper manners, to greet adults with arms folded while bowing, but their tongues were frozen and out of fear they could not utter a single word. Their aunt reminded them of their manners.

"Say hello to *Bác Cả*," the literal translation is Oldest Uncle.

The children looked at the light green floral tiled floor as they bowed and greeted their uncle in unison.

"*Dạ thưa Bác Cả!* – Hello oldest uncle."

He reached out and patted them both on the head like two puppies and said, "*Giỏi lắm, hai cháu ngoan* – well-mannered children, two good kids."

The pleasantries continued until they were escorted by the maid to their shared bedroom. On the way, they saw Khải with their suitcases and ran up to him to hug and claw at his legs like two scared kittens running from water. He said goodbye to them and promised to bring their parents and siblings with him soon. He saw the disapproving looks shooting out of the mistress' eyes. He knew he was a servant and the closeness he showed the children went beyond the boundaries of propriety, but he did not care. He was an orphan himself and his compassion for these children overwhelmed him. He was a simple man and could not understand how their parents could allow this to happen. At the age of twenty-seven, he himself was still struggling to understand how his mother could also abandon him at the age of five.

They were taken to their bedroom to settle in before dinner. Once the bedroom door closed behind them, Tuân hugged his sister and started to cry. He said he missed Maman and Papa and he wanted to go home. Ngoại wiped his tears and nose with the bottom of her dress and told him everything would be OK, even as she herself was also crying. They huddled in the darkness under the sheets in the bed. They held hands and waited until they were told what to do next.

That evening, small vegetarian imperial rolls were served along with grilled pork balls, pungent fish sauce, thin rice noodles and fresh lettuce along with a variety of mints and herbs. Aunt Bạch Nga arranged a small plate of imperial rolls as an offering to the ancestor's shrine to thank them for blessing them with two children. She lit three sticks of incense with a match and watched as the tips of the incense lit up brightly in the dim room. She blew out the flames and held her palms together in prayer position, holding the incense sticks between her fingers toward the sky. She held her hands at her temples and mumbled her thanks and asked for blessings from the ancestors. Then she moved her clasped hands up and down three times to finish and stuck the three incense sticks in a large brass urn filled with dry rice. The children glanced at the incense every once in a while to see the ash curl and wind down around the sticks. Unbroken ashes meant the dead had paid you a visit – that was how they signaled you that they had stopped by to enjoy the treats you offered and would ensure your prayers were sent to the heavens. If the ashes stayed intact and did not break off, your prayers would be answered.

If burning incense would help me win this round, I would have burned a thousand sticks and smoked out the *Sliced and Diced* studio.

"Let me introduce you to our fourth, guest judge today, Chef Martin Yan!" Peter announced.

Chef Yan, wearing a white traditional Chinese coat and lime green scarf, walked out from behind the glass doors leading into the studio. With his hands clasped together, he nodded, a humble gesture so unlike typical American celebrity chefs who wave or raise both hands to claim their air space.

I almost jumped up and ran screaming toward Chef Yan. Chef Yan! He was the world renowned chef who brought Chinese food to mainstream TV. He had hosted his own award-winning cooking show, *Yan Can Cook*, since 1978. I had watched his show on PBS since I was a little girl. I first learned the word "julienne" through him as he demonstrated how it was done with his incredible and swift knife skill, using his cleaver. Mom and I used to laugh as we watched him slam his big knife on the cutting board, smashing garlic, then smile at the camera with his huge grin and proclaim in his heavy Chinese-American accent, "Look at this! If Yan can cook, you can too!" His comedic timing and simple cooking technique were easy to understand, even for those whose English was limited. He was the beloved chef in our household when we did not even know who Julia Child was. He had that Asian quality that Mom and I could easily identify with. Having my idol in front of me threatened to be simply too much. I almost forgot to do one last quick, mental review of what I was going to say for my on-camera presentation.

The camera zoomed in on Chef Yan as he spoke in his usual sharp, quick tone and Chinese accent, "Good luck, contestants!"

Peter saw my wild gaze and was kind enough to give me my cue.

"Kieu, you have three minutes. Are you ready to present your dish on camera?"

"Yes!" I almost shouted.

I wanted to impress Chef Yan with my knife skills, but alas I had already chopped everything, so I had to focus instead on being memorable with my charm and eloquence.

"Action!" said the director

"Hi, I'm Kieu, and today I'm preparing for you another simple *VietnamEazy* dish that will make your taste buds feel like royalty!" I said, smiling confidently. "*Nem*, or Vegetarian Imperial Rolls! What's unique about these rolls is the wrapper. I'm sure you've seen rice paper used in fresh spring rolls, but by frying them, we will change their texture and give them a melt-in-your-mouth lightness and crispiness you have never experienced before."

I picked up a dry rice paper to show the camera and then folded the sides together to break it in half.

"I'm breaking the rice paper in half because we are going to make a miniature version of these imperial rolls. During ancient times in Vietnam, the royal family was often served small dishes, so everything was usually bite size."

I made a gesture with my thumb and index finger to show the small size while looking at the camera.

"Let's now quickly dip our rice paper in a warm water bowl and place it on a cutting board covered in cheesecloth or a thin towel so it can absorb excess water, like so."

I gently placed the wet rice paper down on the cutting board. With a teaspoon I scooped my filling and gently placed it in the center of the half rice paper lengthwise.

"Now fold in the sides, then roll the bottom up like a burrito."

I smiled at the camera.

"Careful not to put in too much stuffing or roll them too tight, as the stuffing will let off steam and expand during the frying process. If you wrap them too tightly, your rolls might explode and make a mess in the frying oil," I said, showing a gesture of explosion with my fingers while smiling.

I continued with my childhood stories. I knew the judges liked that.

"When we were little, we got to eat the ugly ones that did not meet Grandma's quality control. Only the prettiest ones were served to our guests and elders."

I gently placed the roll into the hot oil then picked up the already finished plate. There in the middle of a medium-size square white plate was a small, golden brown fried roll snuggling cozily inside a bright green butter lettuce leaf tucked with a sprig of mint. Next to it was a small blue dish with a light brownish red soy dipping sauce with a little chili.

"Fold up the lettuce to make a wrap and dip it in our homemade vegetarian soy sauce," I said, taking a bite.

I heard a light crunch and was thrilled. Let's hope the sound man caught it! I closed my eyes to savor the moment and tasted the amazing rolls I had just made. Take that Mr. Bacon Man! I opened my eyes and looked up at the camera.

"Um, so good!"

With an endearing smile and thoughts of Ngoại, I added: "So treat your family and friends like royalty tonight and serve them some Vegetarian Imperial Rolls. I'm Kieu, and I look forward to making all your meals *VietnamEazy*!"

Trust

SOUR FISH SOUP
Canh Chua Cá

This soup is distinctive of South Vietnam, where food is abundant. It's a dish that will take your taste buds on an amazing journey of sweet, sour, salty and oh-so-refreshing.

4-6 Servings

INGREDIENTS:

2 tablespoons vegetable oil

6 minced shallots

2 cloves minced garlic

2 tomatoes, cut into wedges

1 pound catfish fillet (basa fish) or red snapper or shrimp

(Traditionally, we use the whole fish, heads and tails too.)

2 teaspoons fish sauce or 1 teaspoon salt to taste

2 teaspoons sugar

1/2 cup tamarind juice or 2 tablespoons paste with white vinegar or lime.

10 okra, cut into 1-inch pieces

1-2 cups pineapple chunks

(Continued on next page)

3 cans vegetable stock or water
1 cup bean sprouts
2 large celery stalks cut into 1/2 inch diagonal slices

If you want to trek into a Vietnamese/Chinese market to find additional ingredients:

A few sprigs of ngò om (rice paddy herb), chopped
2 large stalks of bạc hà (Vietnamese taro stem: It looks like the elephant ear plant, but it is not! We use this instead of celery as the taste and texture is completely different.)
1 small container of pre-fried shallots as garnish

In a five-quart pot, heat vegetable oil until hot, add 3/4 of minced shallots and all the garlic and sauté on high heat for one minute. Add tomatoes and sauté for two minutes. Add everything except for the celery and bean sprouts into the pot. Fill the stock pot with vegetable stock until all ingredients are covered. Add water if needed. Once the soup boils and the fish/shrimp is cooked (about fifteen minutes), remove the protein from the pot and set aside until ready to serve.

Add fish sauce and/or salt to taste. Simmer the broth for another ten minutes.

In a separate small pot, heat 1 tablespoon oil to fry the remaining shallots. Taking care not to burn them, fry until golden and crispy. Remove shallots from oil and drain on paper towel.

When ready to serve the soup, heat it to a simmer, add the protein back in along with the bean sprouts. Turn heat to high, and once the soup boils, instantly remove from heat. Serve in a large bowl and garnish with shallots and chopped rice paddy herb. Traditionally, we remove the fish from the soup at the table so it doesn't overcook in the steaming broth. Serve with steamed rice and hot chili pepper in fish sauce for dipping the morsels of fish.

Taking home the win felt fantastic. The judges loved my imperial rolls and my on-camera presentation. I was reminded that tradition is not always a bad thing. Grandma's recipe of vegetarian rolls not only helped me win, but it put me neck and neck with the likely top contenders – Todd, Deepti and Jay. When I was called to the judges' table I knew I was safe, yet the idea of winning only brushed across my thoughts gently. Because of my fear of disappointment, I did not truly expect to win, despite what I told the camera. When they announced I served the best fried spring rolls they'd ever tasted and reminded me I had immunity for the next round, I wanted to jump out of my ballet flats. But I only smiled, bowed a little and thanked the judges humbly before heading out of the room.

I felt sorry for the cupcake girl, Miranda, who was eliminated. The judges did not find her Chicken Pot Pie Cupcakes cute or amusing, or, for that matter, palatable. Rumor had it that Gnarles spat it out into his napkin and wiped his tongue clean of any residue. Helen, who was devoid of any personality except for her red hair and freckled pale skin, was also eliminated for her overcooked steak. That was her second time at the bottom so we all knew she had to go.

I was so well trained to retain my composure at all times that even if my spirit wanted to soar and scream for this win, it was muted beneath years of practice to suppress any extreme emotion. For us, any overt expression of happiness, even swaying to music, was considered inappropriate, especially for girls. If we were at a dance party or wedding, we were only allowed to move to the music if we were up and on the dance floor. While sitting at a table waiting to be asked to dance, we had to look as if we were at a lecture hall. A slight smile might be approved, but direct eye contact with a man was frowned upon. If a girl were to sway back and forth while in a sitting position she would be labeled *Con gái không đàng hoàng*, a girl with questionable morals. I had seen many girls, inspired by the music, tap their feet beneath the table. It was natural to want to express it. So they contained this excitement somewhere below their ankles.

I saw this repression less in American night clubs when I went out with my girlfriends. I found myself judging my friends when they danced lewdly. Usually I stood back, away from them, as if to say to anyone who might be interested, "I'm not associated with them." These critical thoughts often sent me into a state of confusion. Why were my immediate thoughts disapproving of my girlfriends? Weren't they just having fun and not hurting anyone? Didn't I know them to be wonderful women? I couldn't quite justify my harsh judgments, but my paradigm was so firm it knee-jerked me immediately into that space. It wasn't until years later that I finally threw off those invisible chains. The marks left by them slowly faded from my flesh and spirit, but after so many years their imprints could still weigh me down.

Ngoại was married off at sixteen. Mothers-in-law in Vietnam were like step-mothers in Cinderella stories across all cultures. They were notorious for doing evil deeds to their daughters-in-law and making their lives miserable. If you were lucky you might get one who was polite to you in your presence and criticized you only behind your back. There was a phrase *Mẹ chồng nàng dâu*, mother-in-law daughter-in-law, a simple phrase that only listed two societal roles but carried with it thousands of years of oppression, misconduct, pity, abuse, mockery and excuses for all conflicts between two women. The most devastating mother-in-law criticism started with "I really love my daughter-in-law, but…." That was always followed with a string of stinging complaints.

I was the luckiest of them all. From my first husband, I inherited a mother-in-law who cried at my wedding, exclaiming how happy she was to receive me into her family and for me to call her *Mẹ* (Mom) in front of all our friends and relatives. Her exclamation made me cry tears of joy. I flung away all the discord we had during our engagement. All the petty arguments between a girl of twenty-four and a grandmother of fifty-one on wedding details seemed unimportant to me now. In that moment I completely forgot tradition and freely expressed my happiness by leaping into her arms to embrace her and welcome her into my heart, which had been shut to all women outside my family so long ago.

Following tradition, the groom's family typically paid for all wedding expenses. The groom would offer his bride the most expensive jewelry that he could afford to demonstrate his worthiness as a husband and bread winner. I supposed if I were a farmer in Vietnam, my family would have received a few oxen and many kilos of rice in exchange for me. When I was a kid they always joked about how many kilos of rice I would be worth one day because of my big eyes. These cordial jokes were usually made by Mom to single older male visitors who glanced my way. It was embedded in our hearts that our worth was held in things offered to our families for our hands in marriage. The concept of self-worth coming from "being who you are" was laughable in the Vietnamese consciousness.

For the wedding, the husband's mother was also to give the bride a pair of earrings to symbolize her stepping into her new role as wife. Traditionally, only married women wore earrings, not girls. To keep up this act, my fiancée, in private, gave his mother money to purchase my diamond earrings. I was aware of this exchange and did not mind. Saving face for our families was more important to me than figuring out who paid for what.

On my beautiful wedding day, June 21, the longest day of the year, my mother-in-law slowly presented and placed two half-carat, F color, VVS1 clarity diamond earrings in my ear lobes while exclaiming how happy she was to have me as her daughter. Multiple camera flashes went off. We paused, smiled and posed for this important moment. She had a little difficulty placing them on me so I helped her. The stones were set in gold studs with screws on the back to forever secure them. I felt the hole on one of my ear lobes tear a little as she forced the earring on, but I didn't care. She loved me and that was all that mattered.

After we came home from our honeymoon, I took my lovely earrings to my jeweler to have them reset into thinner studs that did not screw on so tightly.

"My mother-in-law gave these to me!" I exclaimed as the owner studied my earrings under her magnifier.

She looked at the earrings and then up at my face, which was lit up with pride. I saw a look of surprise or confusion cloud the Vietnamese jeweler's face.

"Oh, good," she said. "I thought you bought them. They are of very poor quality, and I know that you usually don't buy crap from us!" she barked in her heavy Vietnamese accent.

I was stunned, yet kept a smile on my face.

"What do you mean? They're VVS1, F color. I know they're small, but we wanted quality over size." Quality diamonds meant I was assured a quality marriage.

I was offended by her statement.

"No they're not," she said, tossing them back to me as if she were afraid they were going to explode between her fingers. "They're S1 at best."

I was stunned.

"Do you still want to change the studs?" she asked after a long, uncomfortable silence.

"My mother-in-law probably got cheated and got bad stones," I said, doing my best to regain my composure and save face. "Let me look into this."

I was shocked that my mother-in-law, who knew her diamonds well, had pocketed our money and bought cheap earrings. This meant beyond a shadow of doubt that my marriage was doomed. Mom always said it was best to get small diamonds of good clarity because they represented a good marriage. Diamonds full of inclusions carried with them omens of a bad marriage. These two little rocks not only tore my ear lobes apart and gave my ears an infection, they later tore my marriage apart and deeply infected my trust in Vietnamese women.

Bad memories of my first mother-in law inspired my next dish on *Sliced and Diced*. Anger rose up from my stomach to my chest and to my throat, urging me to seek justice, when Peter interrupted my thoughts with his chirping as he entered the room where we were all waiting for our next set of instructions.

"Good morning, everyone!" he said, flashing such a broad grin it looked as if he had to be up to something sadistic.

"Good morning," we all mumbled.

"Are you ready for your next set of instructions?"

"Yes!" Most of us faked some enthusiasm to help Peter out.

"Today, you are going to work in teams of two to create a family-style meal that includes at least two dishes, and they must taste great together and represent each one of you individually."

Not today, I thought to myself. I am not in the mood to deal with another personality, especially not another woman's personality.

"Kieu!"

I was startled to hear my name and snapped out of my bitter contemplation.

"Yes?" I replied while feeling a surge of heat rise from my back to my neck. I hated to be the center of attention.

"You won the last round, so you get to pick your teammate!"

Peter flashed a smile at me and this time it looked real. It was the first sincere smile I'd seen from him. Perhaps he could feel I was a bit out of sorts this morning and was trying to be encouraging. I appreciated his efforts and decided to come back to the competition full force.

"Great, Peter. I pick Deepti!" I said.

Deepti looked happy and quickly shuffled her feet to stand next to me. Even though I would rather work with a man, I knew I had to plan this round strategically. If we had to create two dishes that were cohesive in taste, Indian cuisine would most likely fit with Vietnamese food. And I picked her because I thought she was the best chef in the competition, so we could help each other win. Deepti was given instructions to pick out the next contestant to choose their teammate. And so it went until everyone had a partner. We formed four teams.

"Now contestants, you have one hour to decide on a menu and cook your dish."

Deepti and I turned to look at each other. Suddenly there was a part of me that was terrified that I had paired myself with her. Could I really trust her? Could I trust any woman? I desperately wanted to, and in that moment, I decided to go with my heart. If nothing else, that would make the hour go much easier on me than if I was in my head constantly worrying about Deepti's motives. I was there because of my heart's calling and I would honor that.

After a brief consultation, Deepti and I decided that I would make a Sour *VietnamEazy* Fish Soup to balance out her Chicken Sukha. She told me it was from the coastal Western India region. Though it was a dry dish with almost no gravy, it tasted really nice served with just plain steamed rice. With that we were ready to go and each of us ran to the pantry and refrigerator to gather our ingredients.

I knew I had to substitute celery for *bạc hà* (taro stems) and mint for *ngò om* (rice paddy herb). I found a beautiful filet of sea bass that would allow me to avoid taking the time to clean a fish. But the lack of fish bones to make the soup sweeter demanded compensation. My mind raced as I thought about my mom using dried shrimp to enhance the flavor whenever she made any kind of soup, so I grabbed some large prawns. I peeled and deveined them, then quickly cooked the shells in a large pot over high heat to bring out the deep shrimp flavor. I then added vegetable stock and reduced the heat to medium. I continued to chop my celery, pineapple, garlic, shallots and herbs. Once the water boiled, I let it bubble gently for about five minutes, then drained the broth out to remove the shrimp shells. Now I had my soup base.

I looked over to Deepti and she was grinding spices like mad. I had never seen so many spices in one dish in my life! She had cardamom, fennel, cinnamon, cloves, fenugreek, peppercorns, coriander, cumin, chili, turmeric and I didn't know what else. I didn't even know what the heck a fenugreek seed was. Thank God my soup would be mild in comparison so the judges could see the balance we were trying to achieve.

Twenty-five minutes into the competition, I thought about the steamed rice.

"Did you make the steamed rice?" I asked Deepti.

A look of horror took over her face. Neither of us had gotten the rice going.

"I don't have time to do it, do you?" she asked me.

She had a look of "Please rescue us," or maybe that was my ego interpreting her intentions. I did have a little bit of a heroic side instilled in my DNA, a gift from my mother. Maybe Deepti really meant, "Why don't you do it, you idiot, your dish is simple and mine is not. There's not enough time to cook rice, and if it's raw, then it's your fault and not mine." The duality of my wanting to trust her, yet afraid to trust her, intruded on my thoughts once more.

I had to talk myself off the ledge by finding the positive side to this problem. I had immunity, so I could not be eliminated. I could take the risk. But the biggest issue I had was I didn't know exactly how to make rice without a rice cooker. I'd always been taught to rinse the rice in warm water, drain it, then fill the rice cooker with enough water so that when you point your index finger into the water to barely touch the top of the rice, the water should only reach the line of your first joint. Then press the button and when it's ready, it will automatically shut off. How would I cook it on the stove top? Would I confess any of this to Deepti, who would think I was a total loser? Or would I fake it and take the chance to show the world I could not cook rice?

Deepti was staring at me, awaiting my response.

"You're probably better at making basmati rice than me," I said. "Tell me how you like your chicken cut up and whatever else you need help with and I can do that while you make the rice."

Did you ever notice how the way a person behaves in a high-pressure situation reveals their true character? I guess my honesty and desire to help took over naturally while my cunning side took a backseat.

"Sure," she replied, without any sign of annoyance, but maybe a little surprised that I thought she could cook rice better than me.

She showed me how to cut up her chicken thighs and slice her onions before she flew to the pantry to get some basmati rice. I watched as the drape of her blue and gold sari flew behind her as if she were Superwoman.

Presentation of everything, especially food, was vitally important to Ngoại. It didn't matter if it was a simple meal or an elaborate feast for big celebrations. The way our food was presented always made me feel rich. We served our meals in blue and white porcelain bowls and plates. Cracked dishes were never used – that would suggest something was not perfect with our family or fortune. We'd set the small plates in the center, the rice bowls face down on the plate, napkins to the right of the plate, soup spoons face down and chopsticks on top of the napkin with the tips perching on little chopstick rests.

Our chopsticks, made of dark wood, were always matched and straight. No crooked ones were allowed on our table. The way we held our chopsticks said a lot about who we were as people. Ngoại taught me how to read people by the way they held their chopsticks. If they held them too low, they were stingy. Stay away from people like that. If they held them high, they thought too highly of themselves. Stay away from people like that – they would always try to overpower you. If your index finger stuck out while you held your chopsticks, well that was just bad manners. She used to correct my uncle by hitting his finger with her chopsticks whenever it went wayward. I used my chopsticks in a crisscross manner instead of holding them parallel to grasp the food. For years she and I tried to correct this but to no avail. I was not sure what this habit said about me; she never told me. But perhaps it had to do with being a rebel? Or something bad? Otherwise, why would she bother trying to correct it?

Ngoại usually served three main dishes and a side dish at every meal: a vegetable dish, a salty protein dish, a brothy soup and a pickled side dish to balance out the meal. And of course always some pure fish sauce with cut-up chilies as condiment.

Unlike what I've experienced in American families, we never served ourselves first. Similar to saying "Bon appetit," we'd say, "We invite you to eat." As children we had to invite specific elders. "I invite you, Grandma and Grandpa, to eat, and Mom, and uncles, and aunties." This process was always frustrating to me because I was shy and I felt like everyone was staring at me. I usually mumbled and said the words as quickly as I could. Why did we torture children this way? We taught them to be quiet. I got really good at that. Yet I was forced to speak on command to honor adults. It was like not being taught to stand, yet you better run when it was asked of you.

The highest ranking person had to be served first. Usually it was the man of the house, followed by the eldest son, then the female head of the house and then finally the children. The men were always served the best pieces. How we served was also a big to-do. Usually the highest ranking female grabbed the best and biggest cut of meat between her chopsticks and reached out to set it in the honored person's bowl of rice. It was acceptable to stand up and reach over other people at the table while holding up your right sleeve so it didn't touch the food. It was a ceremonial gesture to be observed by all. The only exception to the serving rule was sometimes the beloved first grandson was served first, followed by a pat on the head and nods from the elders. Minh held this prestigious position so he was often served first because he needed the sustenance to grow big and strong. My favorite cut is the drumstick. Yet even as an adult I have never dared to take that piece for myself during any gatherings and have always offered it to my elders. I don't think anyone even realized or cared about which piece I liked best. Being the youngest girl, I made a habit of being invisible.

Sharing of utensils was not questioned in common households. Sometimes we saw people flip over to the larger, unused end of their chopsticks to access community food and then flip them back to use them to bring food to their mouths. Mom said it was *nhà quê*, peasant behavior, to use both ends of your chopsticks. For formal settings, large serving spoons or chopsticks would be placed in or near the dishes. Small individual dipping dishes were given to everyone at the table. For informal dinners, we all shared a community dipping sauce. It was also acceptable, though not great etiquette, to hold up your bowl of rice if you needed to reach to get more food. But perching the edge of the bowl to your bottom lip and using chopsticks to shovel the food into your mouth was considered vulgar. I did it on occasion when I was alone because it was a lot easier to eat rice that way than with just chopsticks. Simplicity was sometimes irresistible.

The rules went on and on. If you were a guest at the meal, you would always be served first. But you had to refuse this honor by pushing the server's chopsticks away from you toward someone else or back to the server as you profusely and humbly shook your head to show you were not worthy. If you made the mistake of accepting that precious piece of meat, you were forever doomed and labeled an ungrateful and selfish person. Mom used to say that Northerners were the best at this by saying *"Mời mời mà lạy trời đừng xơi* – please eat, eat, but I beg to God you don't eat."

Placement of hands was another important thing to consider. Both wrists had to be on the table showing your hands to demonstrate that you had nothing to hide. In America, it was the opposite, you had to hold both hands in your lap and not put hands or elbows on the table. Slurping noodles at the table, unlike what many Americans believed about all Asian cultures, was not acceptable. We liked things quiet; no slurping and no talking with our mouths full. Perhaps these two rules derived from the French. After all, they occupied Vietnam for two centuries.

I carried these paradigms of judgment with me throughout my life. Before going to visit my family, I had to coach John, an American, on the proper etiquette. He was used to piling heaps of food on his plate and keeping his hands below the table. In Vietnam these acts would produce glares and knowing looks from everyone. I was protective of him and didn't want him to be negatively judged because of his ignorance of these rules. Early in our marriage, I hated watching him eat, because all the glaring signs were there to prove that he was a selfish American. Later I realized that a simple shift in perspective was all it took to change my impression. That type of shift in perspective proved more difficult in other areas of our relationship. We adjusted to each other, slowly and sometimes fitfully, but cultural differences left a lasting gulf between us. We tried to bridge this gulf, again and again, but grew weary of trying again and falling short again. Low-level resentment simmered. We both felt it, but could do nothing about it.

I knew Deepti's and my dishes would go great together, but I felt that we needed something fresh and bright to serve with them, so I started to pickle some mango in lime, sugar, salt and a tiny amount of chili to go with our Sour Fish Soup, Chicken Sukha and steamed rice. Deepti gave me a taste of her dish and it was indeed filled with spices, but the coconut cream she added mellowed out the spiciness. The sauce was thicker than I was used to, but it had a sharp, pungent aroma. Deepti tasted my soup and offered what looked to me like a smile of approval. I was glad I had let my guard down and worked as a team to complete this task together. Now we would see what the judges thought. I ladled the broth and fish and vegetables into a deep large bowl and sprinkled on some mint and fried shallot.

"Complete your final touches, you have fifteen seconds before time is up!" announced Peter before starting the countdown: "Ten, nine, eight ..."

Deepti scooped the perfectly steamed rice into a bowl and inverted it onto a nice plate and I seamlessly topped it off with a sprig of cilantro and a sprinkling of fried shallots.

"Time!" Peter said, and everyone's hands went in the air.

Deepti and I looked at each other and hugged.

"Now contestants, you have ten minutes to work together on a three-minute presentation."

Deepti and I worked out our plan, decided who would go first and how we would work together to present our dishes.

After the fall of Saigon on April 30, 1975, our family had to demonstrate we had no money and were just as common as everyone else so Mom opened a coffee shop right outside our front door.

We had to pretend we were earning money for a living and give the illusion that we were a working-class family. The cafe had four tables, none of which matched, a dozen similarly nonmatching chairs and stools and a tall, rectangular serving table. Mom made her coffee and tea and kept her cups and glasses at the tall table. The cafe did not even have a name. Why bother naming something right outside your door? It was simply called *Quán Cà Phê* (Coffee Shop).

One bright sunny morning, Mom sat down after serving her two male clients. She enjoyed watching them drink their morning coffee and tea. A young Viet Cong walked up to Mom's makeshift coffee shop. He could not have been older than twenty-two, but had a haughty air about him and was decked out in full VC green uniform. He sat down on one of Mom's least stable stools, removed his hat, set it on the table and looked around while resting his elbows on the table. The cafe did not have a menu. It was quite simple, and everyone knew how they wanted their coffee. Mom hated serving VCs. After about five minutes, he was ready to order and flicked his fingers at her, a signal for her to come over. Pointing and flicking multiple fingers up in the air was considered disrespectful and impolite. The appropriate hand gesture would simply happen after one had caught the eye of the waiter or waitress. One would subtly lift one's hand from the elbow and rest. The fact that the VC was gesturing with his palm up and fingers flicking really sent Mom to the edge, but she had to maintain her placid demeanor and quickly pasted a smile on her face and came over to him.

"I would like to order *cà phê giật* (yanking coffee)," he said while looking at the sky as if he were observing a rare breed of bird.

Puzzled, Mom asked him to repeat himself. He became frustrated, turned to look straight at her and repeated himself in a louder tone, as if she were deaf.

"*Cà phê giật*– Yanking coffee!"

Mom was now nervous because she did not want to agitate a VC. He could literally throw her and her entire family in a rehabilitation camp over a cup of coffee. But she did not in all honesty know what type of coffee he wanted so she had to ask him to repeat himself again.

Now he got really upset and slammed his hand on the table, flipping his hat to the ground. She was startled and everyone around her looked up. He proceeded to point at her face.

"*Chị khi dể tôi hả* – Older sister, are you disrespecting me?" he spat at her in his thick *Hải Phòng* (Northern Vietnamese) accent.

She was careful to cast her eyes down to the floor as a sign of respect. It was difficult for her to pull this off, as only maids are not allowed to look into the eyes of the mistress or master of the house.

"I am sorry for my ignorance," she continued softly and calmly, "but would you please show it to me so I can make you the drink you desire?"

He stood up and pointed at one of her customers.

"I want his coffee!" he screamed.

It was so comical to Mom, she wanted to burst out laughing, but she managed to clench her teeth together and restrain herself.

"Ah, you want tea," she said. "The tea is in a bag and—"

She could not finish explaining. That would only humiliate him further and everyone in the café was watching them closely. The young VC looked like a bull as his eyes grew larger. His nostrils flared up and down in rapid movements. She gently smiled at him and put her hands on his shoulders to soothe him and batted her eyes and widened her smile. Mom had a way with men when she wanted to. Even though she was seven years his senior, she still called him *Anh*, older brother, to show him respect.

"Please sit down and forgive my ignorance," she said. "I will bring you your coffee right away."

This was how things were evolving after the fall. Saigon changed its name to Ho Chi Minh City. The sophistication was gone. The economy tanked and the rich cultural life slowly eroded. The elderly and children were reduced to working in the streets to feed themselves. Beggars and thieves were rampant. Good people became criminals, but no one blamed them. That was what hunger would do to anyone.

Deepti and I made a great team. She started her presentation by explaining a little about the region of India that inspired her dish, and talked about the spices. Once she was done throwing the ingredients in a pan, I took over with a big smile.

"To balance out Deepti's spicy and pungent chicken, I decided to make for you today a soup served in many Vietnamese families called *Canh Chua Cá*, or Sour Fish Soup," I said. "Of course, I made it *VietnamEazy* for you by using ingredients found in American grocery stores. You may substitute chicken stock or add any protein you like to this soup and your cooking time should be no more than half an hour."

I looked over at Deepti to signal it was her turn.

"It was really fun cooking with you today, Kieu," she said and smiled confidently. "We infused the flavors of India and Vietnam to make for a great Asian family meal. I'm Deepti and I make Indian food friendly."

"Yes, it was great cooking with you as well. I look forward to showing you how to make Vietnamese food *VietnamEazy*!" I said.

We both waved and smiled at the camera at the same time.

"Cut!" screamed the director, and Deepti and I sighed a deep sigh of relief, then walked back to the waiting room.

We sat quietly and did not talk much while the other teams began tearing each other apart with who did this and who should get credit for that. Culturally, Deepti and I were much closer than if we were paired with other contestants. Quiet confidence was a commonality for us.

"Was the steamed rice cooked?" I asked her, chuckling a little.

"Yes, perfectly," was her gentle reply.

We waited as Peter strutted in and called out, "Deepti, Kieu,

Jessica and Jay please come to the judges' room."

We all stood up and I knew one of our teams had won.

As fate gently stepped forward and put me on a reality show that would change the course of my life, fate surprised Ngoại at the door the afternoon she discovered her husband's terrible secret. It shifted her slight aggravation at her husband for forgetting his keys to utter horror upon learning he had a wife in the country all along. Worse than the feeling of having to share her man, she had lost face. Her rank had been reduced to a lowly second wife. It was not uncommon in those days for men to have multiple wives, but no little girl ever grew up wanting to be somebody's second wife. Not one.

For me, coming second to anyone proved to be especially difficult. The competitive seed was planted deep within me at birth. I had to be the best. In America parents would console their losing child with "You did your best and that's all that matters." In my family being number one was all that counted. If you fell short of that, you had better be ready for the criticisms that followed. If your backbone was not strong enough and skin not thick enough, you might as well end your life because you would never ever hear any encouraging words. Instead, you would be made fun of and chastised because you should have done more and been more. Effort and good intentions were irrelevant. Only results mattered. You simply failed.

Deepti and I were the winning team. Linda turned to Deepti and asked, "Deepti, between the two of you, who do you think should be declared the winner of the round?" The director held up his hand to signal Deepti to hold her answer for a few dramatic seconds. Once he gave her the nod, she replied confidently.

"I think I should win that round," she said calmly, avoiding my gaze. "Kieu didn't even know how to cook steamed rice."

Gnarles turned to me, his face apparently devoid of emotion, although I had the feeling he was raising his eyebrows slightly in surprise.

"Kieu, who do you think should win this round?" he asked me.

I was still recovering from Deepti's knife in my back. I needed a moment to regroup, but there was no time. The judges were waiting for my reply and somewhere the director was lurking, hoping he'd get an all-out cat fight between Deepti and me. He wanted to see the fur fly! This was my TV bitch moment and I knew it. Would I stoop to Deepti's level? Would I throw her under the bus? Would I place a stamp on my Ruthless Asian Chick image for the audience, once and for all? Or would I stay true to myself and my principles of right and wrong and rise above her treachery?

5

Breaking Out of Tradition

FISH IN A CLAY POT
Cá Kho Tộ

Cooking food in a clay pot gives it an incredible roasted quality and umami flavor. If you can find a large clay pot in a Chinese market, cook and serve this dish directly from the pot.

4 Servings

INGREDIENTS:

4 tablespoons vegetable oil

2 tablespoons sugar

1/2 cup chopped shallots

4 cloves of garlic finely chopped

1/4 pound bacon chopped into little pieces

1 pound black cod or catfish cut into 2-inch-thick filets

1 tablespoon fish sauce

Salt and pepper to taste

2 sprigs of green onions finely chopped for garnish

(Continued on next page)

Add vegetable oil and sugar to large pan or clay pot on medium high. Caramelize the sugar until brown, being careful not to burn. Add chopped shallots and garlic and cook until translucent. Add chopped bacon and cook for three or four minutes. Add fish, fish sauce, salt and pepper to taste. This dish does require extra-coarse black pepper. Cooking time will be five to ten minutes. Flip fish over once. Do not stir too frequently once you've added the fish or the filets will fall apart. Sprinkle on green onions right before serving.

Serve immediately with steamed rice.

I thought about all the times I allowed women to be unkind to me and I did not fight back, all because of my Buddhist upbringing. In this moment, I once again faced someone who was forcing my hand. I had admired Deepti for her cooking skills and her gentle ways, and had let my guard down. It was true what they say about how the ones you love hurt you the most. Now I was going to have to find a way to make Deepti regret that she had ever crossed me.

The determination to overcome adversity is intrinsic in nature, seen in everything from bugs to bears, but we Vietnamese take the trait to new levels. We've had to, as a way to survive after being conquered and occupied continuously over the centuries by one group after the next. First the Chinese, then the French, and finally the Americans. To survive with dignity my people created imaginary tales that placed the soul of the Vietnamese above all other races and cultures. We developed our own invisible hierarchies to help lift us above others during the years of foreign domination.

The story goes something like this. Our people descended from a dragon lord, Lạc Long Quân, and a heavenly angel creature, Âu Cơ. They were two mystical creatures with tails, wings and horrible teeth who decided to lie together – after they got married, of course. She then laid one hundred eggs. From these eggs one hundred children were hatched. Naturally their oldest son, Hùng Vương, became the first king of Vietnam.

Brace yourself for the rankings created for the different races (it reminds me of the caste system in Hindu culture). Firstly, we are the best. Yet we willingly share our seat with the Chinese, or Big Brother. We are aware our ancestors came from China. So we give them grudging respect for their undeniably rich culture developed over thousands of years. Naturally, we host big celebrations, such as weddings, at Chinese restaurants.

After eleven hundred years of Chinese domination, the French took their turn and poured their influence into Vietnam starting in 1858. The obvious impact the French left was not only on our food, culture and race but also in our spoken and written language. Quốc Ngữ, our national language, was developed by Alexandre de Rhodes, a Catholic missionary, to translate prayer books and catechisms. He and his colleagues created Romanized scripts from phonetic sounds. What separated the Vietnamese culture from other Southeast Asian countries is a subtle European elegance the French left behind and gifted to us.

After the Chinese and French, the hierarchy continues down to the Japanese, Thai, Koreans, Laotians, Cambodians, Filipinos, Mexicans and Arabs, Africans and children born of mixed races, known as *con lai*. It amazes me how someone of a mixed race gets put down so low on the list as if they had a choice in the matter, as if any of us had a choice. I'm not sure how it is those of darker skin tones somehow always end up at the bottom of the list of prejudices in most cultures. So if our children married or dated someone outside of our race, there would be judgment upon the family's values. Shame can destroy a family in one instant. I've known families who decided to pack up and move away due to shame and dishonor caused by a daughter or son who decided to marry someone of African-American decent.

I knew all about the pain of being categorized. For years everyone put me in a box and assured me my issues must come from not having a father, and as much as this was a cliché, I went along with this theory. But deep down I knew there had to be more to it than that. If it were that simple, wouldn't I have jumped from one man to the next in desperate search of a daddy figure? It was true I enjoyed dating older men who were experienced enough to have left behind the years of finding themselves. They had established careers and had outgrown their insecurities. Being with older men allowed me to explore the depths of the relationships without the usual distractions. Most importantly, I found men my age had little refinement and gallantry in their upbringing. Their parents somehow did not teach them how to treat women properly. I loved watching *Gone With the Wind* and was attracted to Rhett Butler simply because he was my ultimate definition of masculinity. He allowed Scarlett O'Hara to carry on with her ridiculously childish behavior because he had confidence in who he was. I wanted a man like that. In truth, I've observed many women, across all cultures, who want men to be men. I wanted a man who speaks his mind, owns his words, and delivers on his promises. But I never looked to a man I dated to become a father figure. I never had the feeling of needing to overcome some deep lack or longing where male figures in my life were concerned. I like men. I trust men. In fact, I find men to be far more trustworthy than women – and kinder and more predictable.

On the other hand, my distrust of women runs deep and has cut gaping red scars in my psyche, the separations, cracks and lines all manifestations of a profound fear of women. This angst established the foundation of my life. On my first visit with my psychoanalyst I announced to him that I knew I had issues of abandonment, failure, performance and acceptance. However, I told him, I believed these issues came from my mother abandoning me, not my father.

"This is why I am in front of you today," I firmly announced. "I need you to help me make sense of it all and overcome it without medication."

I specifically chose him out of a list of hundreds of psychiatrists my insurance gave me because he was also a psychoanalyst. I did not need to sit for hours recounting the gruesome tales of my sadness. I wanted to learn how and why I arrived there so I could begin to build bridges over valleys I created and then cross over them to ease the path of my life.

Now, facing the judges awaiting an answer from me, I lifted my chin and looked Gnarles in the eye.

"My dish did not require rice," I said, pausing a moment to let the impact sink in, and then moved in for the kill.

"Deepti was lost in her dish. She fell behind and forgot to make the rice. As a good team player, I jumped in to help her finish her dish while she cooked the rice."

I looked at the other judges as I felt Deepti's laser stare out of the left corner of my eye penetrating my left temple deep into my skull.

"Judges, if you ask me, you could say that without me, her dish would not have been completed at all," I added.

My words hit their target like a lioness darting out from behind the reeds to pounce on her prey. I aimed for the jugular.

"You can roll back the tape and see that without my help," I continued, "Deepti's dish would have been unseasoned and incomplete. I am not surprised she had to say she won for the team, because it is expected of her to say that. This is a competition. Even a loser has to say she deserves the win."

I glanced over at Deepti with a look of calm unconcern, all the better to belittle her, but my jaw was clenched and I could feel my hands and feet growing cold as I finished my statement and turned back to face the judges.

"Clearly, the obvious winner of this round is me!" I said emphatically.

Even as the words and their impact settled over the judges, I felt ashamed I had stooped to her level. I should have bubbled with enthusiasm about how well we worked together, told the judges we won as a team, and then let them decide who had the better dish. I avoided her gaze afterward in the waiting room and she tried to avoid mine as well.

"Kieu and Deepti, the judges would like to see you now," Peter called out in his usual gleeful tones before spinning around on his heels to leave the room.

I glanced at Deepti as a camera zoomed in for a close-up of my face. A sudden surge of anger rose within me. In that moment, I could empathize with celebrities who tried to smash the cameras of the paparazzi, even poor bald Britney Spears, in shorts and sneakers, bashing a car window with an umbrella. I wanted to run to Deepti to hug her and say I was sorry for all my terrible words. I wanted her to win if it made her happy. I would take it all back. But instead I clenched my jaw, held my head up, reminded myself I was playing the role of Ruthless Asian Chick, and followed Peter out. My hands and feet were clammy as I stopped on the marker on the floor, under the bright lights, in front of the judges.

"Action!" the director barked, waving his hands.

Judge Linda kept her head down as she spoke, trying not to look either of us in the eye so she could avoid giving away the winner.

"Congratulations again as you are the winning team," she said.

She paused a moment to give each of us a long, slow look, mustering her best poker face. Then she slipped into a smile.

"After much deliberation, we have decided on a winner for this round," she said. "As a surprise and a historic first for *Sliced and Diced*, the winner of this round will also win a trip abroad to her ancestral country to explore and do a live travel segment on cooking in her homeland for our network!"

I was instantly lifted out of my depression. My thoughts raced to visions of what it would mean to visit Vietnam, since I had not been back in thirty years! The camera zoomed in as Deepti and I smiled broadly and looked at each other. I could tell she did not enjoy the edge of tension between us either. Gnarles waited until our giddiness subsided for his announcement, drawing out the moment as long as he could.

"The winner of this round is," he said, and again he let the pause draw out excruciatingly.

"Kieu!"

The judges were sitting right in front of me, but the sound of my name being called came to me as if across a great distance. I felt the same joy as the day I got my first job offer. This win was for Ngoại. To revisit the land of my ancestors was the ultimate reward.

I felt a hand on my shoulder and turned around to see Deepti's face closing in on me, smiling.

"Congratulations," she said. "You deserve it!"

She gave me a big hug and turned around so quickly I did not have a chance to respond. I thought I saw tears in her eyes.

"Thank you," I called after her, trying to hold back my own tears of joy, tears of regret and tears of sorrow for my teammate. I knew how much she would have loved to return to India to shoot a special episode.

Linda interrupted the raw emotions bubbling up by asking me to call in Helen and Christian. I could see the irritation in the producer's eyes as he lived for TV moments like these and wanted to milk it for all he could. I was sure he would have a chat with her later to remind her why she was getting paid. It was not because of her judging abilities.

I was thankful I was able to contain myself. My TV persona as Ruthless Asian Chick would be shattered if I showed any sympathy for Deepti. Somehow I quickly refocused and walked into the waiting area to call the two contestants who would now have to face the *Sliced and Diced* cutting board.

Once the first wave of excitement about my upcoming trip to Vietnam started to fade, I realized I was also scared. Though I had often traveled to Europe and South America, I had avoided Asia, and Vietnam in particular, because of the stories I'd heard from friends and acquaintances, who told of hungry children, poor old women and an unpredictable Communist government. I was especially concerned about getting sick from drinking the water and eating raw vegetables. My flight to Vietnam would be in less than twenty-four hours and we would be there for only five days. I was not sure what would happen to my competitors while I was gone. Would they get a break or would they continue on with the competition without me?

I was introduced to the producer of the *VietnamEazy* segment, Tin, an expert tour guide from Vietnam, who sat next to me in the first-class cabin on China Airlines. I always requested vegetarian meals on long flights. They usually serve me first, which is quite nice, and the special meals are also more tasty. Tin chattered on about the food and where he would take us to film. I was thrilled when he mentioned Quán Ngon, a restaurant in Ho Chi Minh City I'd often heard Uncle Quốc mention from his frequent visits to Vietnam. It's a wonderfully large un-air-conditioned restaurant in the middle of Saigon with decoration reminiscent of Indochina. The waiters and waitresses dress in traditional clothes. The perimeter of the restaurant is lined with little food stands where each "vendor" creates his or her specialty dish. Tourists love this spot since they are encouraged to peruse the stands to see all the dishes being made before deciding on what to order. Everything is served at your table, just as at a normal restaurant. Most importantly, you could rest assured that the standards of cleanliness would be maintained at a high level at this local spot.

I asked Tin if it were possible for me to visit the homes of my ancestors on my father's side, as I had never been to Central Vietnam before. His eyes lit up,

"Really? You still have family in Vietnam?" he said with his thick

Vietnamese accent.

"Yes," I said shyly. "I think."

I didn't know much about my father's family except the little my grandma told me. Mom didn't like to talk about that side. I knew that before 1975 they owned acres of farmland, which my paternal grandmother deeded over to Mom before she left Vietnam. Mom, at twenty-five, refused to accept the deed because she was a young city girl and did not know how to manage farmland and was worried what might happen if the Communists were to find out we owned land. It was frowned upon during those chaotic times to own large estates and properties. Tin was ecstatic at my suggestion and rubbed his palms together as if he were plotting a bank heist.

"Kieu, do you know what this means?" he blurted out.

"That you're going to make me go see them?" I replied a little fearfully.

Though I spoke Vietnamese fluently, I did not quite know what I would say upon finally meeting my relatives. "Uh, I'm your long lost relative and I'm going to exploit you by doing a show about you and how you eat, so make it interesting, will ya?" I thought to myself. At the same time, I could feel the excitement growing within me at the possibility of meeting the other half of my DNA.

"Do you know exactly where they live?" Tin went on as sparks flew from the dark of his eyes.

"I could ask my Mom," I replied hesitantly, wishing I did not mention any of it.

"As soon as we land, you will make that call," he said. "This will make wonderful TV. Tell me more about them."

I told Tin all I knew. Soon he was convinced the segment could grow into a one-hour show, not just a short clip.

My heart skipped a beat when the flight crew opened the door at the gate and hot, humid air rushed into the air-conditioned plane. It was really happening. I grabbed my carry-on bag and headed to the off-ramp. The heat was a palpable presence, like a warm, damp washcloth being lowered over me, covering my face and body in an embrace that welcomed me home. I looked around to find a sea of strange faces, and even though I recognized no one, somehow I felt a deep connection. These people looked like me. They were the same height. Their hair and eyes were the same color. They even sounded like me. The only difference I could see was that I was not as skinny as them. My heart and five senses were singing as I took in and memorized everything I saw and felt. After thirty years abroad, I was finally home.

Our black Mercedes SUV with dark-tinted windows pulled up in front of the Park Hyatt in the center of Ho Chi Minh City, and we were greeted by a swarm of pretty young girls dressed in tradition- al *áo dài* dresses. The hotel was impeccable and met our American standards to a tee. Tin checked us in and I was shown to my room for a brief rest. With our tight filming schedule, we did not have much time to relax and be tourists.

I settled in my cool hotel room and enjoyed the smell of fresh lemongrass oil in the air. I called Mom to find out where my relatives lived. To my great surprise, she had all their contact information. She wanted to know why I needed it, but my contestant agreement with *Sliced and Diced* absolutely forbid me from revealing the truth, so I made up an intentionally convoluted story about the producers requiring all of us to fill out forms listing the names and addresses of every known relative. Mom might have wondered what I was really up to, but I was probably even more curious about how readily she was able to give me the contact information. I would have to wait until later to delve into Mom's secrets.

I dialed the number she gave me and was warmly greeted by my male cousin Thiện. His welcoming voice informed me that I was ar- riving at the perfect time for the First Death Anniversary (*đám giỗ*) of his father, my uncle, a celebration that would take place the next day. I was startled to realize he knew exactly who I was and did not hesi- tate an instant to extend an invitation to me. The first anniversary of someone's death is a significant day in Vietnamese culture, a festive occasion for the extended family to gather for an elaborate banquet in honor of the deceased, similar to Thanksgiving. Of course the women spent all day in the kitchen working hard to prepare the food while the men sat around watching TV, drinking and chatting. The responsibility for organizing the banquet fell to the person who inherited the ancestral estates, typically the eldest son.

We arrived in Qui Nhon by air the next day and were met by a driver arranged by the ever-competent Tin and his team. I was anxious and excited all at once. The driver was local, so he knew exactly where to go. He drove like a maniac, swerving around the swarms of motorcyclists buzzing along in every direction and honking his horn nonstop. Tin peppered him with questions about the area. I admit I enjoyed hearing the driver's Central accent. I could only make out a sentence or two as it was quite heavy and tickled my ears.

I'd had a rough time choosing the right outfit for this occasion. I made sure not to wear anything too revealing or even my super high heels. I wore a green V-neck, knee-length jersey dress and platform sandals. In my mind, I had the impression that my relatives lived on dirt floors and wore leather brown sandals, as in the many photos I'd seen from friends who had visited their relatives in Vietnam. I made sure I had little envelopes of money to give out as needed as gestures of appreciation. I had learned from my mother, long ago, that this was standard operating procedure when one visited relatives and friends in Vietnam. I saved the largest envelope for Thiện, who was responsible for the banquet, as he was my host and the eldest.

After an hour the driver veered off the main road onto a poorly paved alley full of gravel. As we bounced along I rolled down the window to feel the midafternoon heat. The warm, humid air felt amazing to me and I couldn't help but note the contrast from that suffocating taxi ride so many years ago here in my home country, when Mom left Ngoại. The driver stared at me, irritated because I let out the cool AC air and invited dust into his car, but I didn't care. He finally stopped in front of a large gated house painted a vibrant shade of turquoise. I saw three middle-aged men and an old lady standing out in front staring at us with inquisitive eyes. I instantly recognized them as my relatives. The men's facial features carried a stunning resemblance to my brother's face.

The men greeted Tin with warm handshakes while I stood to the side. After the initial awkward moment I realized that it was my job to greet the old lady.

"*Chào Bác, cháu là Kiều ở bên Mỹ mới về* – Hello older auntie, I am Kieu, coming home from America," I finally said, remembering the manners I'd been brought up on.

The three men gathered around me and introduced themselves as my cousins. My two cousins were thrilled to hear my perfect Vietnamese and I was relieved to hear they did not speak with heavy country accents. They invited us into the open living room and offered the crew something to drink. Since I had already explained to Thiện, my cousin, our intentions over the phone, no one seemed surprised to see we were followed by two cameramen.

The older woman, Bác, was the widow, my cousins' mother. She took my hand to show me around my ancestors' home. To my surprise, the home was large, clean and well kept. The floors were spotless white porcelain tiles. She explained they had been the wealthiest landowners of the area until most of the lands were split up and given to party members once the Communist regime took over. She talked about a land deed that went missing so it was difficult to prove how much property our family owned. I believe this deed was last seen by Mom, I thought to myself. Without proof to show the land had belonged to our family, the property was seized by government functionaries and split up among local residents. Because of its sheer size, one could tell the main house was built for a landlord, as compared to the mishmash of smaller homes around it. The sore point for my cousins was that the locals, mostly blood relations, did not speak up and tell the truth, happily choosing instead to accept the choice land for themselves.

The three sons were all married and each had his own individual unit connected to the main house. The compound was built in an elongated fashion, similar to a line of rail cars. Each unit was equipped with a living room, one or two bedrooms, a private kitchen and modern private bathroom and shower. It was not as grand as the estates from the stories Ngoại told of her ancestral home, but it was much nicer than I had imagined.

Bác stopped in a large open room in the central area of the convoy. It faced the main gate and had no front walls. This turquoise-painted room had three large red and gold altars. The largest one, pulled up against the central wall, was decorated with Buddha statues, incense, food and water offerings, candles, red lights and large floral arrangements. The one to the right wall was my grandparents' and uncle's altar. I recognized photos of my paternal grandparents. My grandfather was in his thirties when he passed away, so he looked quite young. Rumor had it that he passed away due to syphilis, but no one could confirm that. The altar on the left wall had to be for Bác's ancestors as I did not recognize any of the photos at all. Once I turned around, Bác handed me three sticks of incense and told me to burn them for my ancestors. I knew this ritual well, so I lit the incenses, bowed three times and placed them in the bowl filled with ashes and hundreds of burnt-out red sticks. I was supposed to pray for the welfare of their spirits in the afterlife or for the health and protection of the living. But I was too nervous to think of anything so I just moved my lips around silently as if I were praying.

We continued as the cameras rolled and Tin reminded me not to worry about translating too much into English. They would cut and paste each segment in later and add in voice-overs. Bác continued to show me the back of the house, where I finally saw the younger generation of women and girls. I slowly approached my youngest cousin's new wife, who was squatting in the corner of an open structure with a corroded metal roof, a yard away from the main house. She had jet black hair, tied low and loose at the nape of her neck, and was wearing jeans, a pink T-shirt with white flowers and city heels. She seemed innocent, obedient and no older than twenty-five. She looked up briefly and smiled at me as I nodded. I watched her as she concentrated on fanning the wood fire pit. She squatted on the cement floor with her knees spread out and no stool to sit on. This was a favorite position of many Vietnamese women from the countryside, *nhà quê*.

After introducing myself, I asked her, "*Chị đốt lửa để làm gì* – What is the fire for?" Though she was much younger than me, I still had to call her "older sister." She outranked me because my father was younger than my deceased uncle.

She shyly smiled and giggled while stealing glances at the camera. "*Mình đốt để chồng mình nướng cá* – I'm making the fire for my husband to grill the fish."

Of course, I thought to myself, she had to put in all the hard work sitting outside in the heat to build a fire, inhaling tons of smoke, while her husband got to claim the glory of grilling the fish later. I chuckled a little as I was reminded that men throughout every culture like to cook over fire, even in this small town in the middle of Central Vietnam.

We proceeded to the large main kitchen built just like the ones we see in America, minus the oven. To my surprise the granite kitchen countertops were not used to make imperial rolls or prepare any food at all. All these tasks were done on large, round stainless steel trays by my female relatives while squatting and hovering on the clean tiled floor. Even little girls were actively helping do something on the floor. Though the kitchen had a sink, the fish, meats and vegetables were cleaned at a second floor faucet that came a foot off the ground. I was confused but did not want to embarrass them by asking, "Why don't you use the counter tops and stand up to save your backs?" I learned later that even though modern kitchens were built to imitate our American styles, many women from the countryside were not used to working standing up and preferred to squat while preparing food.

I asked if I might help them prepare the food. This habit of offering to help in the kitchen was taught to me early on. As a guest in anyone's home, girls always had to offer to help. Girls who did not offer to help were deemed rude and *mất dậy* (unmannerly). Of course, the answer would most likely be "No" – and indeed it was – but I had to ask to be polite. If I were a man, nothing would be expected of me except to sit, chat, eat and be complimented by the elders in the main room.

After we spent a few hours of listening to my family's history, an early dinner was served. We sat around a large, round table set up on the tiled area on the front porch. It was dusk, a cool pleasant breeze was blowing and amazing aromas wafted in from the kitchen. I smelled a mixture of fried egg rolls, catfish in a clay pot, grilled and boiled pork and fish, stir-fried shrimp, steamed rice, fish sauce and shrimp paste. My mouth started to water. Despite being a little jet-lagged, I was ready for this feast. I knew the Americans in the crew would never forget this experience. There were plates and bowls of food almost to the edge of the table. The courses kept coming. The women constantly stood up to clear empty plates and bring more food. As guests, we were expected to sit still and focus on eating as much as we could.

It is traditional in Vietnamese cooking to keep the bones, skin and shells intact throughout the cooking process as they bring added flavor to the food. Eating takes a little extra effort, but some enjoy the work involved. I did not know what to do with my bones so I placed them on the small plate in front of me while I held the rice bowl to eat. As I looked around at my relatives, I realized the Americans and I were the only ones with plates of shells and bones. What did the others do with their bones? Eat them? Then I looked down. I was horrified to see there were paper napkins, bones and shells all over the tiled floor. What was this? I leaned over to Tin.

"Why do they throw everything on the floor?" I whispered, and he politely replied while containing his laughter, "It is normal for folks from the countryside to do this."

He saw my look of horror and embarrassment.

"We never did this in our family," I added, while trying not to judge my relatives. No wonder Ngoại did not want Mom to marry my father.

He nodded with a knowing smile.

"I know, I know," he said, and patted my hand reassuringly.

After dinner, the crew said their goodbyes as I lingered with my family. I wanted to hug them, but I was not sure if this was acceptable for my family. I reached out to Bác first to hug her and she seemed surprised as I felt her small body stiffen. I immediately released my hug and held her hand between my palms. I gave her one of the money envelopes I prepared and thanked her for dinner, filled with promises that I would visit soon. I continued this process with each of the ladies in the family. Unlike other machismo cultures, in Vietnam, oftentimes the women controlled the money in the family. It was easier for me, a woman, to give money to my female relatives so the men did not lose face.

I was happy to see the home of my ancestors, but I doubted I would ever visit again. Despite the natural connection I felt to them, somehow they were too removed from me to truly embrace. Was I being influenced by their Communist Party connections? Many Vietnamese in the countryside joined the party as a means of survival when the Americans slowly lost control of North and Central Vietnam to the Communists. Or was I being judgmental, carrying prejudices toward my father's family drilled into me by Grandma? It was dark as we climbed into our taxi. I could hear the summer bugs chirping in the background, the sky was black and full of stars. I was satisfied I finally met my family in Vietnam. Through the dirty car window I saw them there, waving at us. I leaned back as the car pulled away, closed my eyes and yearned for an imagined childhood in Vietnam. I relived every morsel of my first family meal as the crew's voices faded away in the backseat.

6

Merging of Cultures

STEAK AND POTATO STIR-FRY
Thịt Bò Xào Khoai Tây

A country's cooking often reflects the merging of cultures throughout history. I love this dish prepared by my grandma as a special treat. In America, I found a similar dish in Salvadoran cooking called Lomo Saltado. Their dish is influenced by the immigration of the Chinese into El Salvador. In their version, tomatoes are added and soy sauce is used instead of fish sauce.

3-5 Servings

INGREDIENTS:

1 pound rib-eye steak

1/2 tablespoon oyster sauce

1/2 tablespoon Maggi 1889 sauce (substitute soy sauce)

1 tablespoon sugar

1 teaspoon pepper

4 cloves garlic

1 onion

3 russet potatoes

2 tablespoons butter

(Continued on next page)

2 cups vegetable oil
1 garlic bulb
1 bunch cilantro

Slice rib-eye into thin slices. In a small bowl add oyster sauce, Maggi sauce, sugar, pepper and smashed garlic cloves. Mix well. Add the mixture to the meat and marinate for thirty minutes in the refrigerator.

Peel and chop onion into cubes and set aside.

Rinse and peel potatoes. Cut potatoes into 1/4 inch-1/2 inch cubes. Parboil the potatoes. This will ensure thorough cooking when fried, resulting in a soft middle and crispy outer texture. Add butter and 2 tablespoons of oil to a frying pan. Heat until fat is bubbling. Place a layer of cubed potatoes into the pan. Be very careful not to splash yourself with the hot oil. Fry for four or five minutes. Use a large spatula and turn potatoes over gently at least once or twice during cooking. Cook until all sides are golden brown. Drain the fried potatoes on paper napkins to remove excess oil. Sprinkle pepper on potatoes.

Take the rib-eye out of the refrigerator and remove from marinade (reserving remaining sauce for later use).

Heat a fry pan on high and add 3 tablespoons of oil. When the oil begins to smoke, add the rib-eye and onions to the pan. Cook for three minutes or until all edges are brown, then add the marinade back into the pan to create a sauce.

Add potatoes to pan and cook for two minutes. Place on a serving platter, garnish with cilantro.

Serve immediately with steamed rice.

Not until I found myself stowed away in my aisle seat on the flight from Ho Chi Minh City back to San Francisco did the dizzy intensity of those days begin to ease up. I replayed scenes from my whirlwind experience of my home country. I had not been in Vietnam long enough for my body clock to adjust, so while there I stayed on West Coast time and would often wake up at 4 a.m. Rather than fight to get back to sleep, I would slip out of bed and stroll through the park near where I was staying. Those early-morning walks were my favorite times in Vietnam, freed of the well-meaning but intrusive presence of my producer and TV crew. I cherished the chance to have simple intimacies with my people.

To my amazement, I saw groups of men and women in Western workout clothes doing Zumba, ballroom dancing and some form of tai chi. They intently followed the instructor's direction, but I had to laugh, hearing the teachers' singsong voices, a way of speaking I'd never heard in my native language. It was like hearing rap in Vietnamese. I shook my head wonderingly and walked on, smiling at the strangeness of it all and curious what I'd see next. There were also individuals doing random exercises that went against every rule regarding proper form, such as locking one's knees while twisting and bending back and forth, holding a railing while swinging one's legs up and down without any core control. I had to fight hard to hold back the chuckles. I wished we could do a TV show on "How to Be a Proper Vietnamese in Vietnam" and show all the comical things I'd seen on the trip. It would be as funny as the Fung Brothers' "Things Asian Parents Do," which I loved to watch on YouTube, and ring just as true.

Strolling the streets, I almost got run over by a young girl who ran out of a fancy salon with a wad of newspaper that was on fire. She threw it to the ground and jumped over it three times back and forth, then stamped out the fire with her feet, leaving a pile of ashes on the sidewalk. She seemed upset and was murmuring something under her breath. My curiosity overcame my shyness.

"*Em làm gì đó* – What are you doing?" I asked her softly, hoping I would not offend her.

She glanced up at me, a bit surprised, but softened her look and smiled at me.

"*Xui xẻo* – Unlucky," she said. "I had an awful first client to start my day so I had to burn the bad luck away or my whole day will be ruined."

"Why did you jump over the fire three times?" I continued.

She was surprised my Vietnamese was perfect.

"Jumping over the fire will cleanse away bad energy," she said. "Three times is what I am told would do the job."

I think I asked her the questions because I hoped she could help me understand my own past. Whenever Ngoại came back from a funeral, she too would jump over a fire before coming into the house, so she could be sure the deceased person did not follow her inside. As a girl I'd had a hard time understanding why she did that. Now I was starting to get a better idea.

It was impossible not to think about how different leaving Vietnam felt this time compared to when I left the country at the age of eight. I remember being told by Ngoại that we were going on a large plane to France. Though her words were full of excitement, her eyes revealed fear, confusion and sadness. She said we could only bring one of our favorite toys. We were to give away the rest to our friends as souvenirs so they would remember us for years to come. I was upset to have to give away my favorite toys. What about my little kitchen set? My seven dwarfs made of soft plastic? What about Snow White? Actually, I didn't care for the plastic Snow White with a grotesquely large head, so I misplaced her somewhere. I sat in front of the seven dwarfs deciding their fates. Who would be able to go with me to Paris? I chose Bashful. I felt a deep connection to him, to his soft expression, shy body language, yellow coat and sad eyes. He would need me more than the others. The decision to split up his family was a difficult one for me, but Grandma said I could only have one so I obeyed.

On the day we had to leave, it was eighty degrees and humid and Mom dressed me in three layers of clothing, including thick and heavy hand-crocheted sweaters. I had never worn any jewelry in my life, yet that day I wore two gold necklaces, clip-on earrings and bracelets. At one point I looked over at my brother, who also had necklaces on him, and we both burst out laughing. Mom was irritated but too frazzled to make a fuss.

Before leaving the house, Ngoại silently cried as she walked around every room and kissed every table and chair and wall as we watched, quiet, transfixed and uncertain. Neighbors waited outside our front door to say their goodbyes. Our precious black cat with white paws was handed over to our neighbors across from our house. I was excited to get all this attention, yet was confused as to why everyone was so sad. We were going on an adventure, they told us. I saw my little neighborhood friends cradling my dwarfs in their arms, watching me with their dark eyes, tanned skin and bare feet. Their names have faded into the shadows of my mind.

Several cars took my grandparents, aunt and uncles, Mom and us to the Tan Son Nhut airport in Saigon. After the sad goodbyes, I sat in the car between Mom and Ngoại. Mom prepared herself for what was ahead by putting on her tough mask. She held her head high and looked straight ahead. She carried a brown purse that was almost as big as me. Grandma started to mumble a prayer as I watched her legs shake up and down. I put my right hand on her left knee as if to reassure her that everything would be fine. I don't think she even felt my touch. She looked straight ahead as if in a trance, and the shaking continued.

Just as my car sickness started to creep up and I was getting antsy with all the warm clothes, the car stopped. We were at the airport. We unloaded the car and I followed behind Mom. We passed through many security checkpoints until finally we reached a young official who stared straight at Mom.

"*Chị kia, ngừng lại đây* – Older sister, stop here!" he said.

Her quick steps came to an abrupt halt and she turned around to face him. He looked about twenty-five, clean cut and slender. He had to secure his belt tight to hold up his ill-fitted green pants. Mom suddenly remembered her charming smile and walked over to him in her high platform wooden heels. We all stopped in our tracks and turned around to watch the scene unfold in front of us.

"*Trong giỏ Chị có gì thế* – What is in your bag?" he barked at her in an irritated tone.

"*Đồ của phụ nữ thôi* – Just feminine things," she slowly replied while appearing bashful, nonchalant and natural.

I felt Grandma's nails digging into my palm as she firmed up her grip. I looked up at her and saw little beads of sweat appear on her forehead. She was wearing two layers of clothing.

"*Chị mở ra cho tôi xem* – Open it so I can see!" the young man barked.

Mom unsnapped her bag and dumped its entire contents on the table. Perfume bottles, makeup brushes, blush, mascara, lotions, tissue paper, tweezers, scissors and toiletries all spilled out onto the table. So did feminine pads.

The guard was so embarrassed at the sight of feminine pads, he was overwhelmed.

"Chị làm gì vậy Tôi nói Chị mở ra thôi! Dẹp đi – What are you doing? I only asked you to open it. Put it all away!" he yelled at her.

Then he waved his hand to let her – and all of us – continue on. We were all too stunned to react. We could not believe my mother had taken such bold action. My right hand was going numb from Grandma's grip. All I could think of was getting on board the plane and being able to peel off some layers of clothing. Even with legal departure papers in hand, we still had to pass through several more checkpoints. I now understood why everyone on the plane held their breath until the wheels lifted off from the runway. I was confused but thrilled as the roaring hand-claps and cheers filled the plane. Every Vietnamese man, woman and child on that Air France Flight 253 on February 2, 1981, was leaving their homeland to escape the Communist regime. We flew to a mysterious destination where language, culture, food, people and weather were completely foreign, with an allowance of only one suitcase per person, an ounce of gold and a five dollar bill. Our suitcases, specifically ordered by Grandma, made of thick woven wicker, were filled with photos and memories of an era now ended, of life, as we knew it, now over.

Back in the U.S. after my return for more *Sliced and Diced* filming, my heart was not in the competition. Standing next to my rivals, waiting for Peter's next orders, I felt none of the adrenaline rush such moments had brought me before the trip. My thoughts kept racing back to the smells and sensations of Vietnam. I decided to wear summer wedges along with my light blue, floral chiffon dress, and the cold studio air made me regret my decision. My feet grew colder by the minute. I wanted to pretend I was still in Vietnam and I couldn't do that with cold feet!

After spending five frantic days in my homeland traveling, filming and tasting all the different dishes, I realized that one day I would have to go back to the country of my birth and experience living there – not just visiting, but a deeper experience. I was glad that by avoiding ice and brushing my teeth with bottled water I did not get sick, though I wondered if my body still carried vestiges of the all the germs from my childhood and if my system would have been able to tolerate a surge of concentrated bacteria. I was yanked out of my daydream by Peter's British accent.

"Contestants, are you ready for the next elimination round?" he called out.

"Yes!" we replied in unison, all six of us.

"Today, you will be cooking a dish that demonstrates the moment that changed your life."

He paused and looked at our faces to see if he needed to explain further. The remaining contestants looked startled and confused so he smiled and cheered us on.

"Create a dish that has deep meaning for your life!" he urged everyone. "Be creative and cook from your heart! You have forty-five minutes to make it happen!"

"Ready? Set. Go!" And with a wave of his arm we were off into the *Sliced and Diced* refrigerator and pantry to claim our ingredients.

I detested this part most, the running and jostling, the elbowing and glaring at each other. It reminded me of going to Vietnamese stores, where there are no real lines and everyone just cut right in front of you. I never understood it. After years of education and exposure to other cultures, we still shoved and jumped in lines as if the apocalypse were imminent and we would all die of hunger if we weren't first in line at the check-out counter. When I went to places like Huong Lan, a carry-out restaurant in Little Saigon in San Jose, I found myself patiently waiting for my turn when inevitably an older, short woman in ill-fitting shoes and fake Louis Vuitton bag would cut right in front of me. I was taught to respect my elders, so for a while I put up with these transgressions, but after it kept happening time after time, I had to adopt the same behavior or wait in line forever. I was always irritated by their actions. But now I understood it was simply a cultural difference.

I reached for the rib-eye steak as Jay leaped in front of me, stepping on the tips of my toes. He quickly apologized while I used my monkey-like grip to grab the prized thick steak and flew past him before he finished his sentence. I continued to maneuver around my competitors to gather all my ingredients. I decided to get creative in this round and grabbed some tomatoes even though the original recipe did not call for them. My dish was an East meets West steak and potatoes stir-fry because it marked the most important moment for my family.

As the plane took off and soared toward its cruising altitude we were finally allowed to get up out of our seats, and Mom grabbed her huge bag from under her seat. She dug around, finally pulled out two lotion and perfume bottles, and then discretely unscrewed one of the tops. She used a nail file to pull off the plastic cover inside one of the round wooden tops. Mom smiled proudly, shoved the cap in front of Grandma and waited for her reply. She looked as if she were a four-year-old toddler showing her mama a prized toy.

"*Trời đất ơi! Tại sao mày lại làm như thế? Vì mày, mà cả nhà có thể bị bắt hết*! – Heaven and earth! Why did you do that? Because of you, our entire family could have all been arrested!" Grandma cried out, grabbing the cap full of sparkly diamonds.

Mom looked stunned by Grandma's reaction. She let out a silent sigh and turned away from both of us to face the aisle. I could feel the weight of her sadness, even if at that time I could not begin to grasp the depth of it. As I look back now, I imagine Mom longed to get Ngoại's approval. She took big risks to get it, but to no avail.

The gap between them stayed wide my whole life. My mother would never receive the acceptance she desperately needed from her own mother, let alone any compliments. I harbored great hopes that a similar divide would not exist between my mother and me, but it did. I too longed for my mother's approval and encouragement. I too wanted her to accept me as I was and love me despite my dark skin and scarred knee, despite my strong personality and my wrong choices. Her disapproving gaze inflicted countless beatings on my spirit that left it unable to soar. Would I be the one to put an end to this self-perpetuating cycle of abuse? Is "abuse" too strong a word to use for neglect, carelessness, indifference and thoughtlessness of a mother toward her child?

"Kieu, you will have sixty seconds on camera to describe your dish," the director said gently.

I nodded. I was in a daze, filled with sadness. I closed my eyes and waited to hear the director's voice again.

"Five, four, three, two, one, go!" he exclaimed.

I inhaled and opened my eyes with a huge smile.

"Thank you for joining me today," I began, then faltered.

I was at a loss for words. My chest felt heavy and tears blurred my vision. Oh, no, not today. The psychoanalyst warned me this might happen from time to time, and told me to allow myself to let go of the emotion when it did. Not really an option here, however. Instead, I had to work through the sadness. Somehow. I swallowed the emotion as best I could.

"My dish today is Steak and Potato Stir-Fry," I continued, my voice quivering. "It is inspired by our family's migration from Vietnam to France. I imagine the French brought potato to Vietnam and this is one of our family's favorite dishes."

I placed the onions and garlic in a pan as I spoke. The timekeeper man was giving me a thirty-second signal. So I threw the fried potato, marinated beef and tomato all into the pan while frantically stirring, but I was so off my game today. The dish I had made earlier for the judges to taste was a sloppy, brown mess – the added tomato left the cubed meat steamed instead of seared. A rookie mistake I would normally never make.

The next think I knew, I was sitting in the waiting room waiting for the judges to call us in. Todd kept asking me if I was OK and hugged me. I hated hugging, but it was somewhat comforting today. I let him put his long, beefy arm around my shoulder as he sat next to me waiting for the judges.

"You did all right, don't worry," he gently whispered in his deep voice.

He might have been an actor at times, but I could tell these words were genuine. Allowing others to see me weak was a foreign sensation to me. Not because it felt bad. But because it felt good! So I let go and allowed the tears to flow. All the hopes and dreams of getting Mom's approval flowed away with them, onto Todd's pink shirt as he turned me around to hug me and pat my head.

I was a grown woman now. I was responsible for my own feelings, good or bad. My mother was done raising me. That had all ended years ago. I could no longer blame my mother for my unhappiness.

"Kieu and Jay! Please come to the judges table," Peter intoned, startling me with his booming voice, full of authority.

I was not surprised to hear my name called, however. I was sure that between Jay and me, one of us would be sliced that day. Jay made a grilled red snapper fillet on top of quinoa and sweet potatoes. The twist was he cooked the quinoa in tequila to represent something about his twenty-first birthday celebration in Las Vegas. He would not reveal more details to us and kept quoting "What happens in Vegas …" with an impish grin.

I squinted under the blinding studio lights as Jay and I stood uneasily in front of Gnarles, Linda and Peter, awaiting the verdict. I imagined being in a torture chamber where I was interrogated by a guard pointing a bright flashlight right into my eyes.

"Jay," Gnarles began. "Do you know why you are called to judges table today?"

The director gave a hand signal telling us we needed to pause before continuing. Jay had a hard time waiting. He was so anxious to spit out his answer that he started to rock back and forth on his heels.

"Yes, I believe I have the dish to beat today," he blurted out.

The director held up his palm to signal Jay to pause again. Jay pressed his lips firmly together and continued to sway backward and forward. The motion was so exaggerated and jerky, it reminded me of the glass toy filled with a red liquid that moved back and forth on my desk at work. Dippy Bird. I noticed that Jay's bright green tie flapped like the tail of a Vietnamese garden lizard, which almost made me smile, but I was too busy thinking. His pronouncement made me wonder. I scrutinized the judges' faces in search of subtle cues. Could Jay actually have been right? And if he were right that he had one of the best dishes, then didn't that have to mean that so did I? Now it was my turn to be grilled.

"Kieu, do you know why you're called in here today?" Linda asked me.

I was too emotionally drained to debate whether to tell the truth or make this a memorable TV moment for the audience by pulling out my alter ego.

"Because it was one of the worst dishes I have made on the show," I said, finishing with a loud sigh.

I stood with my back straight and calmly looked back at Linda, who flashed me a kindly half-smile. It was a lot easier to be truthful than having to pretend to be someone else. I felt the same relief I did in Vietnam, the same feeling of home. I suddenly realized something else. Home was not a location. Home was not being with people. Home was how I felt about me. Home was me. With that thought I found a genuine smile for the cameras and judges as a warm sensation flowed through me.

Peter was irritated at my smile, saw an opportunity to go on the attack, and pounced.

The show needed drama because drama brought the ratings. Nobody would be cut any slack in that pursuit, and I was the perfect target for Peter's bark today.

"Why are you smiling if you think you made the worst dish?" he asked sharply.

He cocked his head to the side and squinted, all the better to belittle me. At that moment it did not matter how he might feel about me personally. This was all about performance, all about creating moments that would grab viewers and, if the network were lucky, perhaps even trend on Twitter. They didn't call it *Sliced and Diced* for nothing. But I didn't care about any of that, not then. I held my smile even and looked back at him calmly before answering.

"Because I did my best," I said brightly, reciting the typical American answer, which on one level was a total lie, since I could have cooked a better version of the dish in my sleep most days, but on a more fundamental level, in fact my words conveyed a deeper truth, given my long and difficult journey of self-realization and the epiphany the day had brought me.

"Well, I wouldn't smile if I were you," Peter snipped, giving me a final dirty glare before turning back to Jay and breaking into a smile. His sudden turning away, with the cold disapproval it conveyed, gave me a brief flashback to childhood agony and the cold disapproval that was so often my fate, but this time for a change the feeling only lingered for a moment. That really had been an epiphany! Something really had changed for me deep down inside.

"Jay!" Peter cried gleefully. "Congratulations! You made the best dish today!"

And with those final words I knew my fate was sealed.

7

Sweetness of Life

CARAMEL FLAN
Bánh Flan

Flan is a popular Vietnamese dessert. It was brought to Vietnam by the French during colonial times. We love this dish. I prefer to eat it fresh out of the oven, but it is mostly served cold.

4-6 Servings

INGREDIENTS:

1 cup sugar
6 large eggs
3 cups whole milk
1/2 teaspoon vanilla extract

Preheat oven to 300 degrees.

In a large skillet over medium heat, cook one-half cup of sugar until melted (about twelve minutes). Do not stir. Then reduce heat to low and continue to cook, stirring occasionally, until syrup is golden brown (about two minutes).

(Continued on next page)

Quickly pour the syrup into a ten-inch round soufflé dish, tilting to coat the bottom; let stand for ten minutes.

Whisk remaining sugar and the eggs until sugar is dissolved. Add milk and vanilla then whisk until smooth. Slowly pour over syrup.

Place the soufflé dish in a larger roasting pan. Pour boiling water into roasting pan about halfway up the side of the soufflé dish. Bake for fifty-five to sixty minutes or until center is set (mixture will jiggle). Remove soufflé dish from roasting pan. Place on a wire rack and cool for one hour. Cover and refrigerate overnight.

To serve, run a knife around the edge of the flan and invert onto a large rimmed serving platter, reserving the caramel still in the soufflé dish. Cut flan into wedges or spoon onto dessert plates, and top with reserved caramel.

I was not surprised to be sent packing after my Steak and Potato Stir-Fry disaster. It would have been amazing to win, but I was also set to go home, although I was hardly ready to face Mom and hear her "constructive" criticism. Despite my newfound confidence, my fresh understanding of how unnecessary it was to feel I always needed my mother's approval, I knew it would take years of practice to turn this awareness into a habit. At least I would not have to confront her with my failure to win the show until it aired sometime in October. I'd almost made it to the semifinal round, missing only by one dish, and I had somehow created a cooking segment from my trip to Vietnam. That was a huge accomplishment that still had me pinching myself with disbelief. Every time I thought about it again I broke into a smile.

On TV, when they sent a losing contestant home all you saw was the disappointed one leaving the studio or trudging through an airport lugging their suitcases. In the real world of *Sliced and Diced*, being sliced meant you were sent to a small trailer outside the studio where legal counsel sat you down to drill you on the nondisclosure agreement. Only then were you allowed to leave.

I was going to miss my fellow contestants. We said our goodbyes with the usual hugs, teary eyes and sad commentaries, all of us understanding that we might in some way stay friends, but no one knew what that really meant. Perhaps we would stay connected on social media and see pictures and updates from each other's lives from time to time, or just as likely, within a few years we'd let all our links fade until we disappeared completely from each other's lives. I was used to sloughing off old friends. My family moved around so often in the years after we left Vietnam, I could not recall the names of any of my childhood friends before the sixth grade. I learned young to adapt and accept new situations, skills that, for better or for worse, have prevented me from ever becoming too attached to any place or to anything or anyone.

My final meeting with Gnarles had been surreal. He was not only one of the judges, he was also the producer of the show and looked the part staring at me from behind a large, imposing white desk. He was flanked by two stone-faced men in expensive dark suits who could have been anything from hit men to tax accountants, their expressions were so grave and inscrutable. Gnarles motioned for me to sit down and the two men in dark suits found their way to a large red couch. I felt far too emotionally drained to care much about what was going on, but it seemed clear based on the tone of the meeting that I was in some kind of trouble. Had I violated one of the many clauses of the dense *Sliced and Diced* contract? The familiar childhood fear of having done something wrong squeezed my stomach once again. To that point in my life, I was still often seized with that sensation whenever any person of authority summoned me. I found myself wishing that John were with me. Yes, he was emotionally unavailable, but his stolid manner came in handy. I wasn't shy about letting him handle difficult situations like this.

I was fifteen years old the first time I experienced being cast out from my clan. Somehow I knew I was forbidden from dating anyone until further notice. It was never discussed. It was simply assumed.

Girls who liked boys were considered bad. Girls who dated boys were considered inappropriate. I did not quite understand at what age dating would be deemed OK. The expectation made clear to me was that I would get married after college, have children and continue on the path set before all of us. Somehow I also assumed I would marry the first person I ever dated, or I would be considered ruined. I was not sure how these specific conclusions entered my young mind, but I didn't have to understand any of that: All that mattered was the imprint carved deep into my belief system.

Still, the natural urge to go on dates tugged at me. I had the attention of several boys at school, but the one who intrigued me most was no schoolboy, but a twenty-two-year-old Vietnamese man. On Thursdays, carnations dyed shades of green and blue were sold at school and the boys would often present me flowers. I hated the public spectacle of it, felt awkward, and wanted to disappear every time it happened. There was nothing romantic or endearing about it, not to me. It was contrived and torturous, especially going through the ceremonial "Thank you" and "It's so nice." Adding to the misery, I had to carry the flowers around all day to demonstrate my appreciation and my warm feelings for the boys, as if they had marked me for the day. Yes, I'll admit, there was one aspect of the charade I enjoyed – the envious oohs and aahs from the other girls – but that shallow sense of satisfaction was fleeting.

Even later, when dating men as an adult, I disliked being given flowers. Here you were, being picked up somewhere, and they hand you a flower. What are you supposed to do with it? Do you leave it in the car? Turn around and go back inside to put it in water? Carry it into the restaurant? Wouldn't it wilt if it were not placed in water immediately? Seriously, to this day, I despise this gesture. Yet Vietnamese men adhere to this dating rule with few exceptions, a habit they learned from one another, I suppose, not from any woman.

The age difference between me and the twenty-two-year-old Vietnamese man was not much of an issue in our culture, unlike in

American society. However, there were issues with his profession, his education and his height. He was not a college graduate and stood barely five foot four. I met him at a holiday party where he was in the band, playing keyboard and singing. He caught my attention by singing the most beloved Vietnamese version of the song "Papa." As he sang, he kept glancing my way every now and then and each time he did, a warm feeling swept over me. I did not find him physically attractive, but the beauty of his voice overshadowed all his shortcomings.

After months of sneaking in late-night phone calls with Van, I decided to meet him one day after school. I told Mom to pick me up after school a few hours later than usual. My story was that I had to make up a swim session for PE. I wasn't in the habit of lying to Mom, and figured this sketchy assertion would do the trick. When she asked why I had missed a session, I realized that when you concoct a lie, you need a back story to go with it. After a brief moment of panic, I told her that I had left my bathing suit at home in the dryer one day. She frowned at me for my forgetfulness. Maybe this lying thing wasn't so hard after all.

I was thrilled to meet with my music man. Van picked me up after school and we spent two happy hours together before he drove me back to school before Mom would arrive. I was still high from our romantic interlude, sharing ice cream and juice in a local café. He was pulling up to the parking lot to let me out when suddenly out of nowhere in a slow-motion blur I caught sight of the shining glare of the hood of a car speeding toward us. I heard a loud "Boom!" and the whole car shook with the force of the collision and rattled me out of my high. I had never heard nor felt anything like that before in my life. After I woke up from my momentary daze, I noticed the door of the other car open and out stepped Mom. She had rammed the driver's side of Van's car!

"Get out of the car!" she shouted at me in Vietnamese.

I looked over at Van and he looked back with frantic, wide eyes.

He was wedged into the car where Mom's car had smashed against his door and could not get out. I was still looking at him when my mother yanked me out of his car.

"Leave my daughter alone, you hoodlum!" she shouted at him, slamming the door shut.

My head felt like it was about to explode. I bolted away, still enmeshed in a nightmare of profound confusion and dismay, and started to walk inside the school for no particular reason except to get away from Mom. She followed behind, assaulting me with her shouts and insults.

"I can't believe I raised such a daughter!" she screamed. "One who follows boys! One who lies to me! One who sleeps with boys! One who has thrown away her entire future gallivanting around with uneducated hoodlums!"

Her endless name-calling came at me rapid-fire. I felt as though I was trapped in a raging flood and as in the worst sort of torture, the water wouldn't stop rushing and flowing over me. I was drowning, but somehow my legs carried me forward, away from her. I'd managed to grab my school bag out of the car and I grasped it now as if it were a life preserver. Mom finally caught up to me and grabbed my arm and spun me around. I was still stunned by the raw violence of the crash and its aftermath. My brain had not caught up with what was happening. I could hear the loud echoing din of car smashing into car. When my mother's hand reached out with a swift lightning strike and landed against the left side of my cheek, I did not feel any pain. My entire body was numb. It was the only time in my life I had ever been slapped.

Mom dragged me by the arm while school kids stood around agape. They were as shocked and frozen as I was. She shoved me in the back seat of her blue Thunderbird, where my youngest brother sat, and Minh stared at me from the front seat. Neither of them had their seat belts on.

Mom threw the car into reverse and backed away from Van's

car, suddenly freeing him. He jumped out of his car then just stood there, not knowing what to do next. Mom sped past him, running over his left foot. I saw him grabbing his foot and hobbling and looking at me with puzzled eyes before we rounded a turn and he was out of view. Mom's barrage of words spat out continuously. She informed Minh she would take all my savings away from me as a form of punishment. He sat and listened without saying a word, nearly as stunned as I was. As an adult I have often wondered what went through his mind as the three of them sat in the car waiting for me that day, but I never asked him.

We arrived home and Mom ordered me to go inside with my little brother and wait for her return. She was going to the bank and would bring along Minh to help translate. I was relieved to finally have silence. I looked at my little brother, who was only six years old at the time, and hoped he would not remember any of this. He went to the living room and turned on the TV. Chef Yan was on, teaching his audience how to julienne carrots in his usual funny manner, explaining everything in his charming, engaging accent. As a family, we all loved watching cooking shows and there was something both weird and soothing about Chef Yan carrying on happily while life exploded around me.

I went to my room, put my school bag down on the floor and slumped over on my bed, waiting for the guilt to settle in over me. But I did not feel any guilt. Instead a strange new sensation came in its place. I could not feel the usual shame of having done something wrong. The familiar smell of fear did not even sneak in. Instead, the swell of injustice overwhelmed my entire body. My fingers started to grow cold and my body shook. I felt a strong conviction that a deep wrong had been done to me, a conviction that grew into anger. What had I done that was so wrong that I deserved to be slapped and humiliated in public and called hideous names usually reserved for prostitutes? Mom risked not only the lives of Van and me by ramming into us at high speed, but also her own life and the lives of my siblings, her children. How could this be right?

I did not know what to do. I had no relatives nearby to turn to and no friends to run to. My childhood was so isolated from my peers that I did not have a single person to confide in during my hour of need. I felt lost, drowning in thoughts of despair, and was startled when the dark green phone on my desk rang.

"Hello?" I said reluctantly, assuming it would be Mom and not wanting to talk to her.

"Kieu?"

It was Van's familiar, calm voice, now tinged with a hint of panic.

"Can you talk?" he asked me.

"Yes," I whispered.

"We have to run away!" he blurted out. "She will not allow us to be together."

My mind raced with all the rules of proper behavior that had been impressed upon me. Running away with a boy would definitely ruin my life and reputation. That was an indisputable fact. Yet any fear I might have felt was overwhelmed by a deep sense of injustice done to me. Van urged me to make a decision. Mom and Minh would be back soon. I did not have time to weigh my options, to ponder or agonize. My gut would make the decision.

"Yes, come pick me up now," I said in a low and mature voice, firm and decisive. "She's at the bank and will be back soon."

I felt bad leaving my little brother home alone for the short period of time until my mother came back from the bank. The overwhelming responsibility I felt toward all my siblings made it hard to leave. But Mom had forced me into this. She had left me no other option. Throughout the six years living with Mom and away from Ngoại, I had slowly grown a backbone. It may not have been made of steel, but it was strong enough to withstand what happened to me that day.

I believe every child has a seed within him or her. It is a parent's job to nurture and nourish that seed so that it may grow into whatever tree or flower it was intended to be. That seed should be watered, fed, protected and guided, but always allowed to be free to become what the universe intended it to be. To squash the seed, to force the child to become someone else through guilt and restriction, is an act of violence against a fellow human being and contrary to the order of the universe. This is a wrong that many Vietnamese parents continue to perpetuate to this day.

Van drove for two hours, at least, heading nowhere in particular. Neither of us said much. I cried a little, because I was a child beginning to realize the enormity of what I had done. I asked Van to stop so I could find a payphone and call my Mom. After only a few hours, I already missed my family terribly. I wanted to call her to tell her I was OK. I was sure she would plead for me to come home. Once I'd heard her apologies, I would drag it out, pretending to be reluctant, and then grudgingly agree to come home that night. I would have taught her a lesson and everything would be all right once more.

We stopped at a gas station. My fingers trembled as I slowly dropped coins into the slot of the rotary public phone. Van stood next to me to offer support, but by then he was as afraid as I was. He was starting to realize that since I was a minor, he could go to prison if my parents reported him for kidnapping or statutory rape.

As I dialed my home phone number, I felt each pulse in one ear and the beating of my heart in the other. My fingers grew cold as I waited for Mom's phone to finally ring. Tiny ants crawled from the base of my spine up to the nape of my neck.

"Hello!"

It was my stepfather's harsh voice, but I did not want to deal with him now; this was between me and Mom.

"Bố, please let me speak to Mom," I pleaded.

"No, she doesn't want to speak with you," he continued in his harsh voice. "You have upset her. You have made her sick. You better come home."

I was stunned yet again! He spat at me without a single note of care or sympathy for the barbaric way I'd been treated. Now she wouldn't speak to me? The depth of sadness and disappointment I felt then at my own mother was indescribable, and the dislike I had for my stepfather sunk roots into my heart.

I hung up the phone without answering him. Tears welled up and my chest felt tight, but no tears came. I pushed them down, buried them deep. My whole world collapsed with the realization that I was alone and unloved. Worst of all, I had to finally let go of my childhood dream of having a caring mother. I did not ask for her to be perfect, but I did expect her to care. That was her duty. Now I realized I may have come from her seed, but that did not guarantee me a place in her heart.

"Well?" Van asked me, looking pale.

I slowly shook my head in defeat and motioned him toward the car. He opened the door to let me in.

"Let's go to my parents' house," he said. "You can live there. It should be OK. They'll talk to your parents."

At fifteen, I ran away from home with a man. That at least was what they all wanted to believe. The truth was at fifteen I ran away from my own mother.

A few weeks later Mom and Van's parents negotiated the terms of my move back home. I knew moving home was the best choice for me. Living at home would allow me to finish college, get a job and then leave forever. I knew the terms and consequences, but accepted them, because by then I had a clear objective for my life, one that would no longer depend on a mother's love. I served out the sentence for my sins and wore the scarlet letter dutifully for years to come.

Soon after I was eliminated from *Sliced and Diced*, it was time for Ngoại's seventy-fifth birthday. In our Vietnamese culture, this was a major occasion, the *Lễ Thượng Thọ*, or ceremony of the upper life, an opportunity for children to honor and thank their parents for raising them. My family planned a huge reunion in Paris and my mom's youngest sister was in charge of putting together the grand celebration. It was the first time in thirty years we would all be under the same roof.

I was looking forward to seeing everyone, even Mom. The two weeks in Paris passed in a blur of long family meals feasting on unbelievable amounts of food, nightly karaoke and ballroom dancing barefoot in Uncle Quốc's living room. I usually didn't participate in the dancing, but enjoyed watching my family have fun. Mom and I had a good time together so long as we did not discuss anything she deemed unpleasant. At times, I wanted to leave Mom alone and never see her again, but something about blood and family always kept me nearby. But being close to Mom was similar to being trapped in a cage with a tiger: You never knew when the tigress would strike again, so you gently maneuvered yourself around her and wore a lot of padding, just in case.

The second week we were in Paris everyone else was out and about and Mom and I were antsy and wanted to visit a few bakeries. Being alone with Mom was nothing I chose lightly. I appreciated any happy moments I had with her, but there had been precious few of those over the years. After I graduated from college I moved to California to get away from her. I always felt uncomfortable around her and the invisible space separating us was a source of persistent pain, but I did not know how to erase that distance.

During those days in Paris, I sensed her aging more each time I saw her. This made me feel some sympathy, and softened me enough to allow a little space for tolerance and forgiveness toward her. Or maybe that was just how it worked with family: Sheer exhaustion led you to bury the bad and put it behind you. Good then drifted into the picture, of its own will, and you did your best to shape it into something that might last. Despite the shortcomings of our relationship, I was feeling more of a sense of ease and confidence around her, less like a child who could never please her mother. Perhaps I was putting into practice my new belief, the *Sliced and Diced* epiphany, that I no longer needed Mom's – or anyone else's – approval.

She and I loved French pastries more than anything. At the time, Lenôtre was considered the best, so we puzzled out the right subway route and found our way to 44 Rue d'Auteuil. The aroma wafting out the front door of the bakery was intoxicating. The glass window displayed an unbelievable array of petits fours, pastries and cakes. We bought two boxes of goodies for the family to share later that evening. My favorite was always baba au rhum, a light cake soaked in rum with an amusing name. We strolled to a nearby cafe to stop for an afternoon drink and snack.

It was a cool day but the sun was shining just enough to keep us warm. We sat in the small, typical wicker French chairs and placed our treats on the small iron cafe table. Mom ordered her usual cafe au lait and I, crème de menthe. We ordered a baguette, pâté de campagne and flan dessert to share.

I sat facing Mom and waited for the familiar sensation of space opening up between us to descend. But to my surprise the atmosphere remained comfortable, intimate yet relaxed. Could it really be happening? I squinted through the sunlight, studying my mother's face while she looked absently out toward the street. Could our mother-daughter relationship really be evolving into a casual friendship? As we enjoyed our drinks and smooth, creamy flan, I debated whether to risk destroying the moment by asking a question. With Mom it was always hard to predict how she would interpret any given thing at any given time. A probing question might seal this new closeness – or shatter it.

I was once told, "Whoever sees the problem is responsible to fix the problem."

I saw the problem, the open wound that we shared. I wanted to heal the wound, once and for all, so I could move on with my life. After Mom and I chit-chatted about the visit and gossiped about my aunties, I met her eye and lowered my voice.

"Mom, I have a question I've been meaning to ask you," I said, speaking deliberately and tentatively, as if I were a child sneaking up on a house cat to catch it. Her face shifted from enjoyment to confusion and for a moment I wished I could take back my words. But it was too late.

"*Chuyện gì* – What is it?" Mom replied, straightening up.

I could see her shield coming up as she sighed and braced herself for my kicks.

"I just want to know why we never talk about me," I told her, gaining momentum now. "We talk often, yet you only tell me about other people, and never ask me about my life. You never ask about John. You never ask about *me!*"

I was on a roll and a part of me wanted to complete the thought, grab my purse and sprint away from whatever I had wrought. Yet even more powerfully, I wanted to know the answer, even if it were horrible or insulting. I was prepared to move on with my life, as an adult at last, and never look back, if that was the way it had to be. Her eyes narrowed as she spoke to me.

"*Tại vì Mẹ nghĩ Mẹ không có quyền hỏi con vì Mẹ không làm tròn bổn phận của người Mẹ. Mẹ không có nuôi con từ nhỏ* – Because I don't believe I have earned the right to ask you, because I have not been a complete mother to you. I didn't raise you when you were young." She spoke her truth with a soft sigh so powerful, it blew away my wall of judgment.

I was stunned. All those years I thought she did not care about me or ask about me because of the shame I had brought upon her for not being the perfect daughter she demanded. Yet all along, she felt she was not good enough for me?

"You have the right, Mom, because you're my mother," I said, my voice shaky. "Don't ever feel like you cannot ask me."

Her tears began to flow. I reached out for her hand to reassure her. Our roles had suddenly reversed. Now I was the mother consoling her broken child. All the sadness, anxiety and fear that I had carried with me toward my Mom for so long was now replaced with compassion and love. All those years of sadness and pain triggered by her inexcusable actions and words were now vanishing in the fading Paris sunshine. I had learned the truth.

I came to understand that day that the love of a child toward a parent is truly unconditional. At that sidewalk café in Paris I wanted to take on all Mom's sufferings as my own so she could be free of their weight and scars. Some seeds are stronger than others and better equipped to weather the storms of life. Yet we all have merits and were placed here to serve one another. Some plants have to seek out the sun amid the tall trees to live out an extraordinary life. Others want to live in the shadows and remain small to help anchor the roots of a tree. I was an oak tree and Mom, for all her ferocity and bluster, was a dainty flower that could easily be plucked away by a harsh wind. Her parenting might have violated every rule in the book by contemporary, Western standards, yet she had done what she could, with all the heart and soul she could muster, and she had helped prepare me for my extraordinary life.

8

Through Hell

━━✕━━

Hades Rice
Cơm Âm Phủ

Cơm Âm Phủ or Hades Rice is a popular dish in Hue city in Central Vietnam.

Dish 1: Lamb Chop

INGREDIENTS:

1 tablespoon balsamic vinegar
1/4 tablespoon fresh rosemary leaves
1/4 teaspoon fresh thyme leaves
Pinch black pepper
1 tablespoon brown spicy mustard
1/2 tablespoon olive oil
1 lamb chop, about 3/4-inch thick

In a bowl combine all ingredients up to the lamb chop. Pour over the lamb chop and marinate for at least one hour in the refrigerator. Remove from refrigerator and allow the chop to warm to room temperature. This will take about twenty minutes.

(Continued on next page)

Heat grill until smoking hot. Place lamb chop on hot grill and sear for about three minutes on each side. The meat will be medium-rare. For medium, cook for an additional thirty seconds on each side.

Dish 2: Grilled Chinese Sausage

INGREDIENTS:

1 Chinese sausage

Heat grill on high until smoking hot. Grill sausage on all sides for thirty seconds (two minutes total).

Dish 3: Fried Egg

INGREDIENTS:

½ cup olive oil

1 large egg

Heat olive oil in a pan for three minutes on high heat. This might look like a lot of oil, but don't worry; it will make the bottom of the egg super crunchy and the yolk will remain creamy. Crack the egg directly into the hot oil. Cook for one minute, or longer if you like your yolk hard.

Dish 4: Seared Foie Gras

INGREDIENTS:

1 tablespoon olive oil

1 4-ounce piece Foie Gras, ¾-inch cut

Heat Dutch frying pan on high heat for three minutes. Add oil. Cook each side of the foie gras for ten seconds.

Dish 5: Kobe Beef Carpaccio

INGREDIENTS:

3 ounces Kobe beef thinly cut into slices

2 tablespoons olive oil

1 tablespoon capers

A small piece of brie thinly sliced

Fresh ground peppercorn

Arrange Kobe beef on a plate, sprinkle all ingredients on top and serve.

Dessert 1: Beignets (makes about 2 dozen)

Ingredients:

4-6 cups vegetable oil (for frying)
1 cup water
1 cup milk
1 large egg
3 cups all-purpose flour
2 tablespoons baking powder
1 teaspoon salt
2 teaspoons sugar
1 pinch nutmeg
Powdered sugar

Pour oil into a large, deep pot or a deep fryer and begin to heat. Combine water, milk and egg in a large mixing bowl and mix well. Add flour, baking powder, salt and sugar. Mix until the batter is smooth. When the oil has reached 360°F, drop individual spoonsful of batter into the hot oil and fry. Flip over the beignets two to three times until golden brown and puffy, then remove. Drain on paper towels and sprinkle with powdered sugar and serve.

Dessert 2: 1 piece of fresh Durian, that most unusual

Malaysian fruit.

Halloween was always my favorite time of the year. The air was crisp and clean and everyone seemed to be in a happier mood. I was excited to host a party at Mom's house so we could all gather to watch Episode Six of *Sliced and Diced*. No one in my family knew that I would be eliminated in the episode. I hoped it would not put a damper on the night and turn the whole thing into a pity party. I was proud of my accomplishments and thrilled with the experience, but alas no one would believe me, even if I swore it on a light bulb. (Yes, light bulb: In Vietnam, instead of saying "I swear on my mother's grave," we sometimes say "I swear on the light bulb." If we were lying, then some magical curse would cause the bulb to burn out instantly. What was the likelihood of that ever actually happening? Zilch!)

In Vietnam we had our own version of Halloween, though the reason and meaning of our festival was slightly different. We called it *Lễ Cúng Cô Hồn* (Hungry Ghost Offering Festival). The festival fell on the same day as the Buddhist Festival *Vu Lan*, usually in July. It was a day to celebrate and display our piety or dutiful dedication to our parents. Forgiveness was the theme of the day. For one day, the spirits in hell got a break and were allowed to roam the earth to visit their relatives and have some food. I loved how my culture cherished the act of eating so much that we even built in a holiday to allow dead spirits a day to chow down.

Ngoại used to tell me horror stories about what happened to us if we were bad and ended up in hell. I remember lying under the covers with her at night as she recounted the scary tales of Hades. Why were these stories always told at night? My childhood home in Saigon was a large, three-story house. Its steep, dark stairs leading up to our bedrooms were never well lit due to restrictions on the use of electricity after the war. As I crept up the steps each night, I would imagine ghosts lurking in the shadows, waiting for me, and nightmares inevitably followed. I took to racing up the stairs as fast as I could to avoid the lost souls, then would run through the hallway and into the bedroom before diving under the covers. I was glad I shared my bedroom with Minh and my youngest aunt.

These horrifying stories were told to children to make them better behaved. In Grandma's stories, people who lived vicious, nonpious, unkind lives were doomed to hell. These bad souls were cursed to live an eternity in endless hunger, pain and suffering. There were nine stages of hell and the ninth was the worst of all. Souls were tormented by the devil himself forever. One torturous game they played on the hungry souls was placing a delicious hot pot of food in front of them. Then they were given large and long spoons to scoop out the food, only to find the spoons were too long and they could not use them to shove food into their mouths. The devil had a sense of humor. If, however, they succeeded in bringing any morsels of food into their mouths, it would instantly turn into hot coals or lava and burn their throats and tongues.

Traditionally, when a person passed on we put gold or coins in their mouth before the body was cremated. When praying for their soul, we burned paper money, clothing, even houses and cars so they would have something to bribe the monsters of hell with and win better treatment. Bribery, it works everywhere!

During Hungry Ghost Festival, knowing that the gates of hell would open up for just one day to allow hungry spirits the opportunity to eat, we offered trays of rice, salt, water or candy, a process that began with burning incense. After the incense was burned, the trays were tossed onto the street for the spirits to catch, eat and enjoy. Unlike offerings placed on our ancestors' shrines, it was deemed bad form to eat food meant for the hungry ghosts. Kids gathered all around to fight each other for the candies Grandma tossed onto the street. Minh and I were usually confined to our balcony on the second floor, where we would watch the neighborhood kids have fun, screaming, catching and scrambling around to pick up candies off the ground. Ngoại did not allow us to participate in these festivities as she deemed it inappropriate for us to scuffle around snatching up candies like common street kids. She also said the candies were touched by lost souls and would be unsafe for us to eat. Our nannies or maids slipped the candies to us on our own dishes instead. We missed out on much of the fun, but did enjoy watching other kids climb over each other for the treats. In the back of my mind, I was concerned about hurting other kids knowingly by giving them candies touched by dead spirits, but I never dared voice my worries.

We used the episode of *Sliced and Diced* as an excuse to create a small family reunion. After we left France in 1985, family reunions in the States were rare and always cherished by all of us. So as usual, all the women were in the kitchen together. Mom was the boss and we were all sous-chefs. Besides the usual American fare of chips and dip, we also made Rice From Hell, a dish from Hue, the imperial city of Vietnam. This dish was made famous more than eighty years ago by a restaurant called *Âm Phủ* (Hades). It was a rice dish delicately presented with seven different toppings to represent the first seven steps baby Buddha made. On the menu Mom also made Crab in Secret Sauce, Imperial Rolls, Feminine Salad, Sour Fish Soup, Fish in a Clay Pot, Beef and Potato Stir-Fry to commemorate today's episode, and always flan for dessert. I was a little nervous to see how Mom would react to seeing me add tomatoes to the traditional stir-fry dish.

Though millions of Vietnamese had migrated to America since 1975, we continued to prepare our traditional foods without much ingenuity. I had never seen a newly invented Vietnamese dish until my recent visit to Ho Chi Minh City, and I was excited to see the new Vietnam, a country that was progressive, inventive and youthful. For those who refused to return because of the loss and hardship they had endured, I wished they would allow themselves a chance to see the positive changes that had infiltrated the country since President Bill Clinton dropped the ban on U.S. trade with Vietnam in 1994. Or perhaps I was more hopeful because I was not old enough to have experienced the huge loss of adults who left Vietnam during and after the Vietnam War.

I was shredding the cooked chicken for the salad when one of Mom's stories popped into my head – about a funeral she witnessed when she was thirteen years old. Children were usually discouraged from attending funerals. It was believed that spirits were attracted to young souls and might steal or haunt the young person's spirit, bringing illness or bad luck. As the story goes, on the way home from school one day, Mom heard loud cries spilling out into the street. She could not help herself. She had to approach to see what the commotion was about. A funeral for a young soldier was being held inside the courtyard. She could tell the family members from the guests by the clothes they wore: Immediate family members wore white outfits and white head ties similar to Rambo's bandana. These ties had to be torn, not cut, from the same cloth, since they symbolized family ties and cutting the cloth would have been deemed bad luck. The widow and female relatives cried and wailed as loudly as they could, and banged on the coffin each time they asked God why he had cursed the soldier with such a dreadful death.

"Why you, why my husband?" they continued as long as they could.

"You are too young, why are you leaving me with our children. What will we do now?"

Wealthy families were known to hire actors to do the crying to save face for both the dead and the living. They hired "criers" to demonstrate to the world that the deceased would be greatly missed by the family. We asked these actors to say words we could never express directly ourselves to the ones we love. Mom hid behind a tree as she watched the family's anguish.

I was born into a culture that encouraged silence and disdained public expressions of love toward the ones we care about while they are among us. Yet once they departed this earth, we fully embraced all forms of public expression, both physical and verbal, to demonstrate our anguish. During one of the widow's passionate throws being witnessed by my mother, she accidentally tipped over the wooden coffin, causing the lid to fall open and spill out parts of the remains of the soldier, who had died in a bomb attack. Mom recalled the putrid smell and yellow, slimy flesh falling out of the coffin. For reasons unknown, Mom's compassion for the family made her leap up and run toward the coffin as if the dead soldier were of her own flesh and blood. Everyone else, including the widow, watched in horror, paralyzed at the sight of loose pieces of decaying flesh falling to the ground, but Mom carefully picked up pieces of the soldier's body and put them back into the coffin with her bare hands. When she retold the story years later, she said she could still recall the smell of decay and feel of the flesh as if it were yesterday. For months after this most bizarre incident, the odor of dead flesh emanated from her fingers and she was not able to eat her favorite dish, *Xí Quách*, leftover cooked meats and bones used to make beef or pork stock. In that moment Mom moved on impulse without thinking, but the act displayed her heroic tendencies in abundance.

Just before *Sliced and Diced* came on, my family gathered in front of the screen to watch a video I brought back from Paris. It was an old video of *Lễ Cầu Siêu*, the memorial service of Vietnam's last emperor, Nguyễn Phúc Vĩnh Thụy, whose imperial name was Bảo Đại,

Keeper of Greatness. He passed away on July 30, 1997, in Paris. In Buddhist tradition, we prayed for the spirit of the deceased on the forty-ninth day after their passing. It was the estimated time for one's soul to reincarnate into a new life.

Ngoại was honored with the royal family's invitation to recite a poem as a tribute to our last emperor. I was always fascinated with her life. Her father served the Imperial Court so long ago, yet his legacy carried on with her. I was not aware she was in touch with the royal family at all. While I was in Paris she handed me the video after her birthday party to remind me of my roots.

She made me sit down by her side on her bed and recounted tales of her father's burial and also his reburial. The family believed his original burial plot carried with it bad omens. After a string of bad luck for many members of the family, they found a feng shui master who advised them to move his body to a better location to help change the fate that would be bestowed on all of the female descendants in our family. The curse was for us to have incomplete marriages, meaning divorce, no marriage, or worse, becoming someone's concubine. This curse dropped down on a few of her siblings, including Grandma, so in later years she and her siblings had a ceremony to remove their father's remains to a less cursed spot.

Ngoại wanted me to remember the family from which I came. She wanted to remind me that the values instilled in me could not be bought, bartered or recreated in just one lifetime. The strands that twisted our fates together were ordained by something of greater consequence. Despite financial hardships and a broken family life, we would always carry with us, across three continents, this intangible wealth amidst the hell of wars and revolution.

The time finally came for us to gather around the large flat-screen TV to watch Episode Six. This was also my first time seeing the episode. The lawyers reminded me not to reveal the results of the show to anyone, not even family, until after it aired nationally. I enjoyed watching my family's reaction to Jay as he made red snapper with quinoa and tequila. I translated the ingredients to Mom and she made an exaggerated grimace.

"That's disgusting!" she proclaimed.

"Quinoa is for poor folks in Vietnam when they can't afford to buy rice."

That made me chuckle. I also disliked this weirdly textured grain, celebrated by many in California as a "super food," whatever that is, and I was glad she was on my side.

It was so strange to watch myself on TV. I seemed taller and thinner than I thought. The makeshift mask of confidence that I wore now struck me as comical – I knew how I was really feeling inside. I wondered if the audience could see through that mask as easily as I could. During the actual contest, in my mind's eye I was controlled, quick and sharp with my movements. Watching on TV, it was like I was in slow motion. I was cooking next to Bacon Man, who moved quickly and tasted everything he made; he was clearly skilled and more than just an actor, as I had concluded during the taping of the show. He was also a giant standing next to a young-looking, skinny Asian girl with a tightly tied ponytail in a blue, floral chiffon dress. The concentration on my face displayed fearlessness, but when the camera was able to catch my eyes just right, I could see the panic that loomed within those dark irises.

After several commercial breaks and lots of funny commentaries from my aunties on everything from the way the contestants cooked to the way they wore their hair, the moment finally came. I stood to the left of Elvis. My hands were clasped together resting in front of my body, my eyes straight ahead as if I were a naughty school kid waiting to have my palms swatted by the ruler-wielding teacher. Elvis tipped back and forth on his heels and his lips moved slightly but no sound ever came.

"That young kid looks crazy, mumbling to himself," my youngest aunt exclaimed with her thick Vietnamese accent.

"Was he saying something to you and we could not hear?" she continued. They showed lots of curiosity on how the show was filmed.

I honestly could not remember that moment and wished they would be quiet so I could watch myself fall off my horse in peace. I held up my hand to gesture silence so I could hear Peter's comment to me. Though I recalled it being critical, even cruel, it did not sound that way at all watching it now. Did they re-record the sound and dub the scene? Or did I only imagine it that way? It's true what Horace Walpole said about perspective. "The world is a tragedy to those who feel, but a comedy to those who think."

Everyone was quiet waiting for the verdict. To the surprise of every person in the room except me, the show concluded with my elimination. I watched the faces of my family members as they slowly stole glances at me but kept quiet. I could tell they felt sorry for me but were afraid to say anything until I spoke up first.

I looked at them and could not help but smile, which just confused them. They all seemed perplexed that I was neither sad nor disappointed.

"That was a good show," Minh said, breaking the silence. "You tried and that's what matters."

My brother, who has five children, was careful not to be overly critical, in the American way he had learned.

"It wasn't fair," my aunts told me. "We think your dish looked better."

They rolled their eyes and shook their heads as they spoke to emphasize what an obvious and great injustice had been done to me. During the commercial break they took turns offering condolences and words of encouragement, and I appreciated their support.

But I heard nothing from my mother. She was slumped on the sofa in silence. I could only guess what she was thinking. Was she stunned that I publicly humiliated her? Was she disappointed that I could not even give her a heads-up beforehand so she could have prepared herself for shame and ignominy?

I was relieved for her when the commercial break ended and my face appeared on the screen again, this time smiling. I was wearing a bright yellow dress and, I had to admit, looked great.

"Hi everyone, I am your host, Kieu," my face on the screen announced. "I am excited to be sharing with you the magic of my homeland as we travel through Vietnam to experience local dishes and learn unique cultural perspectives within each and every dish. Stay tuned on Sunday mornings at 11 a.m. this spring as we travel through Vietnam, the country of my birth! *Xin chào*!" The clip faded away with some Asian-inspired music in the background and me coyly waving at the camera with a Cheshire cat smile.

My aunties and everyone else in the room jumped out of their seats, clapped their hands together and took turns hugging and congratulating me. Their laughter erupted to replace the solemnity they had felt only moments earlier. They took turns asking me why I did not say something about getting my own show. Mom interrupted my hug with my nieces and shoved her way in to get closer to me.

"What happened?" she asked.

She had a tentative, perplexed smile. She was as confused as a lost child who missed the joke.

"Mom, I did not win the show, but I have my own weekly show instead," I told her. "It is not called *VietnamEazy*. It's called *Xin Chao*."

Mom stayed silent and reached out to hug me, tears in the corners of her eyes. I used to have to reach up to try to hug her so long ago, yet now I had to stoop down a little so she could hug me more easily.

"*Chúc Mừng Con* – Congratulations little one," she whispered into my ear.

Even John had not been aware of my new show. My contract required me to stay silent until the sixth episode aired and even if it would probably have been permissible to let my husband in on the secret, I liked the idea of holding off and letting him see for himself later when he watched the show. Maybe I was a little superstitious. Maybe I still didn't believe it 100 percent either. John was confused about why I needed to go back to Los Angeles every other week after coming home from the competition. I told him we had to shoot more B-roll footage for *Sliced and Diced*, and rolled my eyes talking about the strange ways of reality television. That seemed to satisfy him. I'd thought that coming to a new understanding with Mom after all these years of anguish might have given me a sudden feeling that I no longer needed John, since his role for so long had been to provide the stability and unconditional love that I was deprived of as a girl, but that had not been the case so far. It's a tricky business, trying to guess where your heart will take you. Maybe I did need John less, but in needing him less, I felt more freedom and strength, which in turn gave me the feeling that I could see John in a new way. My life was pulling me forward to an exciting new chapter, and the invigoration of fresh life was either going to bring John and me closer, and revive something crucial between us, or fail to do that. What I knew about John for sure was that he would be truly happy for me, whatever my new life meant for us, and that he, like me, needed time to process what was happening, time to put old realities to rest and open up to the new.

I will never forget my surprise when I was asked to come to Gnarles' brightly lit office after being climinated. I wished I could go home, but was forced to sit there until he brought in those suited men. He introduced the men behind me as the producers of a new show. I was relieved I was not being sued by the producer of *Sliced and Diced* for violating some obscure rule.

"Kieu, this is Gary Walker and Thomas Caddow."

I turned around and nodded. I thought it odd that they remained seated behind me and did not get up to shake my hand. Manners, something the new generation of men needed to learn. Perhaps I could create an app for it. "iManners." For this scenario, they will search, "What to do when someone introduces you."

"Hello!" was all I got out of them. Gnarles seemed irritated at them as well, but continued.

"Kieu, we know you must be disappointed to be eliminated from the show," he said.

As I listened to his words, I quickly scanned around the room to see if there were any cameramen around. I thought I was done with the show. Was I still on camera?

I leaned forward to listen to him as he continued.

"Gary and Thomas saw your *VietnamEazy* travel food segment and they really liked it!" he said.

"Oh?" was all I could come up with. I was still wary.

Suddenly Thomas leapt up from the sofa and rushed past me to lean part of his bottom on Gnarles' glass desk and face me. He smiled, lifted off his sunglasses to reveal beautiful blue eyes, and made his pitch.

"How would you like to host your own cooking and travel show?" he asked me.

I think I stopped breathing for a moment. I looked at him and back at Gnarles and back at him.

"Yes! We can see it!" he said. "You'll travel everywhere, seeking out extraordinary dishes and putting a twist on each one to make it easy for anyone to make. You can have spices and condiments sold everywhere all over across America with the label 'VietnamEazy' or whatever name we want!"

I was stunned and speechless.

Gnarles finally spoke up in his raspy voice.

"What do you say?" he asked me.

The room went silent. I could hear my heart pounding in my ears. I needed a moment to take it all in. My husband usually helped me make these decisions. He was the calm voice I trusted. Today, I had to accept or deny this opportunity all on my own. Then I remembered my own advice to anyone who was out interviewing for a job: "Do what you need to get the job offer, then decide later if you want it or not."

"Yes! Of course!" I cried out.

Then I bounced out of my chair to shake Gnarles' hands.

"Thank you for changing my fate!"

He looked up at me from across his imposing white desk and spoke a truth I have always known.

"No, Kieu," he said. "You changed your fate."

His words were the sounds of a Buddhist singing bowl that started in my heart and resonated through my fingertips.

RECIPE CREDITS

Chapter 1
Sauteed Crab in Secret Sauce – *Cua Rang Sauce Cà Chua*
Chris Yeo, STRAITS AND SINO RESTAURANTS, Houston and San Francisco, San Jose and Burlingame, California

Chapter 2
Feminine Salad – *Gỏi Phụ Nữ*
Khai Vu, LE PHO, Las Vegas

Chapter 3
Vegetarian Imperial Rolls – *Nem* or *Chả Giò Chay*
Johnny Hoang, BLUE SEA RESTAURANT, San Jose

Chapter 4
Sour Fish Soup – *Canh Chua Cá*
Trami Nguyen Cron

Chapter 5
Fish in a Clay Pot – *Cá Kho Tộ*
Trami Nguyen Cron

Chapter 6
Beef and Potato Stir Fry – *Thịt Bò Xào Khoai Tây*
Khai Vu, DISTRICT ONE KITCHEN & BAR, Las Vegas

Chapter 7
Caramel Flan – *Bánh Flan*
Thuvan Hovanky, PHO & GRILL, Maryland

Chapter 8
Hades Rice – *Cơm Âm Phủ*
Tirone Huynh, BIG T's SEAFOOD & BAR, San Jose

Acknowledgements

Thank you to everyone in my beloved family who supported and inspired me on this journey. To my Grandmother (Ngoại) Thi Thinh Nguyen, for raising me and for sharing with me all the stories that made me proud to be Vietnamese. To my mother, Xuan Phuong Nguyen, thank you for teaching me how to cook, sharing with me your adventures, and giving me your sense of humor. To my Aunt Kim Thoa Norton, for reminding me to be courageous. To my Aunt Kim Thanh Nguyen, thank you for being my best friend. To my late Grandfather Tham Huy Trinh, Uncle Trung Viet Nguyen, Uncle Trung Tin Nguyen and Michael Cron, you are the men I look up to. To my step-dad, Vinh Tran, and brothers Kevin Nguyen, Khai Vinh and Tuan Vinh, for inspiring characters in the story. I love you.

To all my supporters from the Kickstarter campaign, I'd like to add a special thank you from the bottom of my heart. Facebook friends and Chopsticks Alley community, you kept me entertained with all your posts and food inspirations. Thank you Dr. Enrico Melson, for always believing in me and for giving me different perspectives. Many thanks to Aleene Althouse and Dr. Katie Griffin for encouraging me during the early phase. Your friendships gave me strength.

To all the chefs, John Le, Martin Yan, Chris Yeo, Tirone Huynh, Khai Vu, Johnny Tuan Hoang and Thuvan Hovanky, my lasting gratitude for your friendship, food and recipes that inspired many scenes in the book. Special thanks to my mentors, Ken Gray and Ron Ikejiri: You changed my life with your wisdom and much needed validation. Thank you Thomas Vo for keeping the lights on when days are dark.

Thank you to my publisher, Steve Kettmann, for your guidance during the early stages of writing this book. Your continued support and encouragement in the importance of sharing a different aspect of the Vietnamese-American story is what kept me motivated. Most of all thank you to the Wellstone Center in the Redwoods for taking a chance on this first-time novelist. To Pete Danko, a skillful and patient editor, thank you for spending so much time reviewing every word again and again – even the recipes! – to help the music in the language reveal itself. Lastly, thank you America for giving us a new life.

ABOUT WELLSTONE BOOKS

We are an independent publisher in Northern California that focuses on personal writing that is not afraid to inspire. We believe that changes in the publishing landscape create an opening for small publishers committed to developing each project as a labor of love, and we insist on taking the time to let a manuscript develop with care and consideration. Our experienced team brings decades of experience to editing and design, and our titles have received coverage in publications ranging from the *San Francisco Chronicle* and *San Jose Mercury News* to the *New York Times* and www.NewYorker.com, as well as cracking regional bestseller lists. We do not accept unsolicited manuscripts, but are always looking for writers who are familiar with our publishing philosophy and want to work with us to develop future projects. Interested writers, or journalists in search of review copies or author availability, write to: **books@wellstoneredwoods.org**

Also Available From Wellstone Books

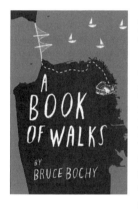

A Book of Walks
By Bruce Bochy

The manager of the San Francisco Giants, having taken his team to World Series victories in 2010, 2012 and 2014, is known nationally for his rare knack for staying on an even keel even in the midst of some very stressful situations. How does he do it? One thing he's always tried to do is get in regular long walks, which help him clear his head and get over the disappointments of the day. This pocket-sized volume, dubbed "an endearing little book" by the *New York Times*, takes us with Bochy on eight talks around the country, each its own chapter (complete with map of his route). Come along for the ride on walks through Central Park in New York, along Lake Michigan in Chicago and across San Francisco to the Golden Gate Bridge. How does Bochy keep a cool head, the Toronto *Globe and Mail* asked?

"In the tradition of thinkers like Rousseau, Kant and Thoreau, Bochy, sixty, swears by long strolls and vigorous walks – 'the freedom to be alone with my thoughts for a while' – which he makes time for wherever he is," Nathalie Atkinson writes.

A Book of Walks, a Northern California bestseller, makes a memorable gift for any baseball fan – or fan of walks.

Kiss the Sky: My Weekend in Monterey at the Greatest Concert Ever
BY DUSTY BAKER

For his eighteenth birthday, Dusty Baker's mother gave him a great present: Two tickets to the Monterey Pop Festival of June 1967, a three-day event featuring more than thirty bands, and use of the family station wagon for the weekend so young Dusty could drive down from Sacramento to the Monterey Bay. He was another young person, trying to take it all in, sleeping on the beach with his buddy, having the time of his life soaking up the vibe and every different musical style represented there. Baker's lifelong love of music was set in motion, his wide-ranging, eclectic tastes, everything from country to hip-hop. He also caught the Jimi Hendrix Experience, who put on such a show that to this day Baker calls Hendrix the most exciting performer he's ever seen. He went on to years of friendship with musicians from B.B. King and John Lee Hooker to Elvin Bishop. This account grabs a reader from page one and never lets up.

"At its best, the book evokes not only the pleasure of music, but the connection between that experience and the joy of sports," NewYorker.com writes.

"Reading *Kiss the Sky* is like having a deep conversation with Dusty Baker – about baseball, fathers and sons, race, culture, family, religion, politics – and always music," says Joan Walsh of MSNBC. "He doesn't sugarcoat anything, but he makes you feel good about being alive nonetheless."

#1 in Wellstone Books' "Music That Changed My Life" series.

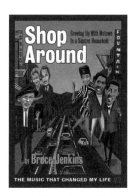

Shop Around: Growing Up With Motown in a Sinatra Household
By Bruce Jenkins

Bruce Jenkins was twelve years old, living in Malibu with his parents, when he heard the original "Shop Around" single, by "The Miracles featuring Bill 'Smokey' Robinson," the first Billboard No. 1 R&B single for Motown's Tamla label. Released nationally in October 1960, the single would ultimately make it into the Grammy Hall of Fame, and for young Bruce, it was a revelation. Jenkins grew up surrounded by music. His father, Gordon Jenkins, was a composer and arranger who worked with artists from Ella Fitzgerald and Billie Holiday to Louis Armstrong and Johnny Cash, but was best known for his close collaboration with Frank Sinatra. His mother, Beverly, was a singer. For Bruce, "Shop Around" ushered him into a new world of loving Motown. In *Shop Around*, he brings to life the first thrill of having the music claim him, sketches from his life with his father and mother, and traces how his love of music has grown and evolved over the years.

"Bruce Jenkins manages to accomplish the always dangerous task of describing music with words as well as anyone I've read," rocker Huey Lewis says. "His knowledge is formidable and his passion is infectious.

"A warm and witty memoir about how music binds us all," according to Joel Selvin, *San Francisco Chronicle* pop music critic.

"An absolutely essential read. An awesome story about a priceless time in music history," adds Emilio Castillo, Bandleader for Tower of Power.

#2 in Wellstone Books' "Music That Changed My Life" series.

Night Running: A Book of Essays About Breaking Through

This daring volume combines the best of writing on running with the appeal of the best literary writing, essays that take in the sights and sounds and smells of real life, of real risk, of real pain and of real elation. Emphasizing female voices, this collection of eleven personal essays set in different countries around the world offers a deep but accessible look at the power of running in our lives to make us feel more and to see ourselves in a new light.

From acclaimed novelist Emily Mitchell and Portland writers Anne Milligan and Pete Danko and authors Vanessa Runs and Steve Kettmann to Bonnie Ford, T.J. Quinn and Joy Russo-Schoenfield of ESPN, a diverse lineup of writers captures a variety of perspectives on running at night. These are stories that can inspire people of all ages and backgrounds to take on a thrilling new challenge. The contributors all have distinct tales to tell, but each brings a freshness and depth to their experiences that make *Night Running* a necessary part of every runner's library - and a valuable addition to the reading lists of all thoughtful readers. We're putting together a Night Running 2 collection; writers interested in contributing should email us at **info@wellstoneredwoods.org** for guidelines.

"A book for anyone who has used solitude and exertion to explore a new crevice of their own mind. Fear, exhilaration, anger, accomplishment, despair, euphoria – every one of these emotions is distilled in *Night Running*."
                                                    – David Epstein, *The Sports Gene*

"A fascinating and eclectic collection! In Night Running, eleven essayists express, with bracing honesty, how a simple act of will—running in the dark—can free body and mind from fear, and restore the spirit."
                                    – Novelist Mary Volmer, author of *Crown of Dust* and *Reliance, Illinois*

"*Night Running* captures in a myriad of ways the essence of running: solitude, self-discovery and the exhilaration of a momentary escape from the banal."
                                    – Sandy Alderson, general manager, New York Mets, 2:53 marathoner

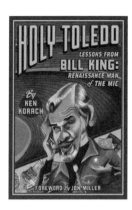

Holy Toledo: Lessons From Bill King, Renaissance Man of the Mic
BY KEN KORACH

Korach, longtime voice of the A's and Bill's partner for ten seasons until King's death in 2005, is the perfect one to bring Bill King to life on the page. A half-century ago, Ken Korach was a kid in Los Angeles, spinning the night dial to tune in Warriors basketball games from faraway San Francisco for one reason: He just had to hear Bill. Now, in *Holy Toledo: Lessons from Bill King, Renaissance Man of the Mic*, he tells the remarkable story of King the legendary baseball, basketball and football broadcaster. Bill was a student of Russian literature, a passionate sailor, a fan of eating anything and everything from gourmet to onions and peanut butter, a remarkable painter. Korach draws on a lifetime of listening to and learning from King – as well as extensive research, including more than fifty interviews with King's family members, colleagues, friends and associates – to create this rich portrait.

Bob Welch
"If I had a hitter I had trouble with, I'd ask Bill how I should pitch him. He always had a good answer."

Greg Papa
"Bill King was the greatest radio broadcaster in the history of the United States."

Tom Meschery
"Talking with Bill was like talking with an encyclopedia.… If you wanted to talk sports, literature – when Bill talked you listened, because he always had something interesting to talk about."

Al Attles
"He didn't sugarcoat it. Bill was a departure from the way it was. If a player from the Warriors made a mistake, Bill told it like it was."

WELLSTONE CENTER
in the Redwoods

The Wellstone Center in the Redwoods, a writer's retreat center in Northern California, publishes books under its Wellstone Books imprint and offers weeklong writing residencies, monthlong writing fellowships and occasional weekend writing workshops; we also host regular Author Talk events. Founded by Sarah Ringler and Steve Kettmann, WCR has been hailed in the *San Jose Mercury News* as a beautiful, inspiring environment that is "kind of like heaven" for writers, described in the *San Francisco Chronicle* as "the kind of place where inspiration seems to just hang in the air, waiting to be inhaled," and featured in *San Francisco Magazine*'s "Best of the Bay" issue. Visit our website at **www.wellstoneredwoods.org** for all the latest on our programs.